KING ARTHUR

AND THE KNIGHTS OF
THE ROUND TABLE

KING ARTHUR
AND THE KNIGHTS OF THE ROUND TABLE

STORIES OF CAMELOT AND
THE QUEST FOR THE HOLY GRAIL

MARTIN J. DOUGHERTY

amber
BOOKS

Published by
Amber Books Ltd
74–77 White Lion Street
London
N1 9PF
United Kingdom
www.amberbooks.co.uk
Appstore: itunes.com/apps/amberbooksltd
Facebook: www.facebook.com/amberbooks
Twitter: @amberbooks

ISBN: 978-1-78274-374-3

Project Editor: Michael Spilling
Designer: Zoe Mellors
Picture Research: Terry Forshaw

Printed in China

CONTENTS

MYTH AND LEGEND

King Arthur is one of the most well-known characters in the Western world. Few people have not heard of his Knights of the Round Table. Their tragic tale has been retold and reimagined countless times – so many times that two people may know versions of the story that contradict each other in several places.

Few of us know where these tales came from, and nobody knows the truth behind them for certain – if indeed there is one single truth underlying this fascinating romance.

Most of us have only a vague idea about the lives and deeds of Arthur and his knights, but can name various key elements. We know that Arthur was a great King of Britain who defended his realm against invaders and foes. We know that his wife Guinevere had a romance with Sir Lancelot, greatest of all Arthur's knights. There was a wizard named Merlin and a sorceress named Morgana Le Fay, and a mortal enemy named

OPPOSITE: **Sir Galahad, the quintessential knight-errant, personified the ideal of the 'gentle Christian knight'. Yet this element was a late addition to the Arthurian mythos; early versions of the tale are quite different.**

Mordred. We know that Arthur was fatally wounded in tragic fashion defeating his great enemy, but did not die. Instead, he was taken away to sleep until he is needed again, leaving the world behind him somehow diminished.

This is perhaps the classic version of the romance of King Arthur, and not all elements of this version appear in other tellings. The origins of this story are complex – a mix of history, myth and the imagination of talented people. Perhaps it is this that makes King Arthur such a compelling figure – he speaks to our sense of the mythic, yet his tale rings with the truth of history.

The classic tales of Arthur and his knights have contributed to the general impression of 'knights in shining armour' that many people have. Movie retellings of the story have helped perpetuate the visual image of the heavily armoured warrior clad in steel plate, wearing heraldic symbols and following a code of chivalry. Yet the reality – if there was one – might be quite different.

BELOW: **In some versions of the tale, the wizard Merlin was thought to be at the birth of the infant Arthur.**

Fact and Fiction

Movie versions of the tales of King Arthur are typically set in what might be described as a Hollywood version of the Late Medieval era, but the classic literary versions vary in their setting. The armour and equipment of the 'knights' (if the concept existed at the time) serving King Arthur would have been very different in the early Dark Ages when some of the tales are set. Arthur's shining knights might have resembled a Norse or Saxon warband, or even something else entirely.

Heroes who seem oddly similar to Arthur appear in other historical sources and in the mythology of people far from Britain. It could be that Arthur's legend is one of what have been described as the 'universal myths' – similar stories that appear in different places without any cultural connection. The reason for this is typically that stories are based upon experience and enhanced by imagination. Most cultures have a story about a great flood, which is not surprising since the majority of humans live close to water.

Similarly, the tale of a heroic leader who held back foreign invaders and had to contend with intrigue and turbulence among his followers may be a universal one. History is replete with great kings, few of whom had a trouble-free reign. Perhaps an 'Arthur story' can be found in almost any culture.

However, it is more likely that today's legends of King Arthur came about as a result of stories being swapped when cultures met and melded. If so, the tale of a great king somewhere in the Middle East might be conflated with one about a lord of the Ancient Britons, eventually creating an altered myth incorporating parts of both stories. Given the attraction of a good tale, chances are these would be the best parts, and any inconvenient historical truths would be discarded.

ABOVE: Sir Lancelot was the greatest of Arthur's knights, but a hero with serious flaws. His sinful nature prevented him from witnessing a miracle at the Chapel Perilous, home of the Holy Grail. It fell to other, more pious, knights to complete the Grail Quest.

Spinning a Good Yarn

Stories often evolve as they are told and retold, and any given writer will inevitably put his own slant on the narrative. A staunch Christian might emphasize Arthur's piety and respect for the Church, while another writer might be more interested in

ABOVE: **An illustration from 'Idylls of the King', a poetic reimagining of the Arthur story by Alfred, Lord Tennyson. This work was part of the modern resurgence of interest in the Arthurian mythos.**

the supernatural elements. Eventually, different versions of the tale will evolve, and this is without considering a deliberate reimagining.

The compelling characters and rich background of the Arthurian legend provide a setting ideal for the creation of new versions of the tale, and any new version might add completely new elements. Mark Twain's 1889 novel *A Connecticut Yankee in King Arthur's Court* introduced a time-traveller whose knowledge of modern technology gave him advantages over the superstitious people of the Middle Ages. Nearly a century later a movie with a similar premise featured a time-travelling astronaut and his robotic companion against the backdrop of Arthur's court.

Stories of this nature are in no way a retelling of the Arthurian legends, they merely make use of the familiar setting as a vehicle for a new story. However, the backdrop and characters are derived from the original tales – albeit rather vaguely – and tend to follow the popular conception of the Arthurian setting rather than making any effort at realism or faithfulness to the original tales.

In recent years, the Arthurian legends have received several different treatments. Some versions have made an attempt to tell the 'real story' of Arthur and his companions, and are based on one of the characters who might possibly be the original Arthur. Such versions have tended to make a credible attempt to portray the look and feel of the era realistically. Thus we see Arthur as something more akin to a barbarian prince than a perfect Christian knight from a strangely clean Camelot.

Other versions stay closer to the popular conception, using a pseudo-Medieval setting complete with heraldry, tournaments and all the usual elements of such depictions. These versions often use the 'default' Arthurian setting because it is familiar to the audience and will therefore need little explaining. If the viewer can make assumptions about the setting, then more screen time is available for drama and character development.

This approach bends the Arthurian setting to the needs of the storyteller, who uses it to tell what is in effect a new tale or at least a new take on the traditional storyline. The TV series *Merlin* is set in Arthur's youth, using familiar characters in new ways to tell a story centred on the relationship between a young Arthur and Merlin.

Any TV show that runs for more than a few episodes will inevitably deviate from, or add to, the stories it is based upon, and in truth, this is nothing new. The story of Arthur has grown and changed since the earliest known versions, and before those there were tales that were adopted into the Arthurian mythos.

Thus the modern legends of King Arthur might be rather different to the tales told about the same characters 10 centuries ago, and the versions told in the future might be quite different to ours. There are historical truths to be found within the various versions, and there are also some epic tales that probably come straight from the author's imagination.

Arthur has often been called the 'Once and Future King', and it is fair to say that his is the once and future legend. The Arthurian romance will be told and retold for generations to come, and it will evolve until it is hardly recognizable. Given how different some of the versions are from one another, it is not unreasonable to suggest that this has already happened at least once.

BELOW: **The gift of Excalibur to Arthur from the Lady of the Lake is one of the best-known moments from Arthur's story. It is not in the original tale, however. Arthur's sword there is called Caliburn.**

1

THE REAL KING ARTHUR

Historians have identified a number of figures who might have been a 'historical Arthur' – someone who defended at least a part of Britain in troubled times and built a realm that was renowned far and wide.

These figures include early British war-leaders, possibly of Celtic origin, a Romano-British cavalry commander doing his best to protect his people after the soldiers of Rome evacuated the islands, and later kings who might more resemble the classic version of Arthur.

There are also traditional Celtic tales that revolve around a figure who looks suspiciously like a proto-Arthur. The mystical elements of these stories are probably the origin of the supernatural parts of some Arthurian legends. Since this traditional Celtic folklore has been a part of Western culture for many centuries, it feels familiar and tends to ring true when incorporated into the tale of King Arthur.

OPPOSITE: The multiple crowns in this Medieval depiction of King Arthur indicate that he was High King over other kings in Britain rather than the ruler of a unified nation in the modern sense.

Thus the Arthurian legend seems to be a combination of real events and mystical folktales, with a fair amount of Christian influence as well. This did not happen overnight; today's many versions of the Arthurian legends developed through numerous retellings and the occasional gritty reboot. Much of the general storyline is derived from a collection of Medieval literature dealing with legendary and semi-historical events in Europe, collectively known as the 'matters' of Britain, France and Rome.

There are similarities between these three literary cycles. Much of the 'Matter of France' deals largely with the exploits of the paladins – a term now generally taken to mean heroic knights – serving Charlemagne in his battles against the Moorish invaders. Most famous of these tales is the *Song of Roland*, a tragedy based on historical events occurring around 778 AD. Roland and the paladins were killed defending Roncevaux Pass to allow the rest of their army to escape.

BELOW: **The tale of Roland (illustrated) and the paladins has much in common with that of King Arthur. It forms a major part of the body of Medieval literature known as the 'Matter of France'.**

Like the tales of Arthur, the *Song of Roland* is a mix of fact and fiction. The battle did likely take place, and heroic deeds were done. Later versions of events introduced the heroic paladins – in some variants of the tale one of them is a sorcerer – until the story entered the realms of myth rather than history. Indeed, the word 'paladin' has come to mean a warrior who is a paragon of virtue, usually a gentle Christian knight or possibly a holy opponent of evil. Yet the original reference was nothing to do with virtue.

The 12 paladins who served Charlemagne were high-ranking nobles whose title probably derived from the Latin 'palatinus', with connotations of rulership. In Britain, some regions were established as semi-autonomous areas whose lord ruled them as he saw fit so long as he met an obligation imposed by the crown. County Durham was a county palatine founded in the early days of the Norman Conquest to defend the rest of Britain from the Scots. Lancashire was set up as a county palatine in 1351.

Thus these paladins were most probably high-ranking nobles with responsibility for regional governorship – which says nothing at all about their piety or character. According to the *Song of Roland* they fought to the last to defend the retreating army, saving many lives by their sacrifice and earning eternal glory. It is perhaps through this combination of self-sacrifice and feats of arms that the term 'paladin' has gained its new meaning. The word, with connotations of heroism and virtue, has been applied to Arthur's Knights of the Round Table, even though few if any of them would have been rulers of a palatinate.

ABOVE: **Roland's battle against the giant Moorish knight Farragut is memorialized on the Palace of the Kings of Navarre. Farragut had only one weak spot: his navel. After a lengthy fight, Roland impaled him there with a spear.**

Although the *Song of Roland* and the associated tales are less well known today than the Arthurian legends, the Matter of France has at times been widely known and extremely popular – perhaps as much so as Arthur's legend. There are some parallels between the deeds of the paladins and those of the Knights of the Round Table, and also between the stories themselves. The matters of France and of Britain are tales of national heroism (albeit from a time when there were no countries in the modern sense) and form part of the culture of those nations.

The 'Matter of Rome' is somewhat different. It is a rather anachronistic retelling of the myths of ancient Greece and Rome in which various Medieval concepts are substituted for historical accuracy. Warriors are recast as knights, with tournaments and other purely Medieval concepts added into the mix. The subject matter is largely drawn from the work of the ancient poet Homer, and it is not at all clear how closely his poems reflected historical reality. He was writing centuries after the events he described, and essentially creating a narrative from old tales he had collected. In modern parlance, the 'Matter of Rome' is a reboot of the classical myths set in a pseudo-Medieval era.

THE 'MATTER OF ROME' IS A REBOOT OF THE CLASSICAL MYTHS SET IN A PSEUDO-MEDIEVAL ERA.

Similarly, the 'Matter of Britain' draws on historical sources as well as traditional tales and a great deal of Celtic mythology. One underlying theme is the arrival in ancient times of heroes from the Trojan War, which features in some Celtic mythology as well as pseudo-historical material dealing with the descent of Welsh nobility from these heroes. In many cases these writings are an interesting mix of known fact and what is presumably invention, with the royal bloodlines running back from people who definitely lived to ancestors who are almost certainly mythical. The exact point at which history fades into myth is unclear.

The 'Matter of Britain' is not exclusively the tale of King Arthur and his knights, although Arthur is of particular importance. In this body of Medieval literature, Arthur is a king of the Ancient Britons who defends his realm from Saxon invaders. The era is the fifth or sixth century AD, some time after the end of Roman rule in Britain, so within the period sometimes referred to as the 'Dark Ages' rather than the High Medieval era depicted in most movies about Arthur.

ABOVE: The Roman invasion of Britain initially met with vigorous resistance from local tribes, but the Britons lacked the unity necessary to prevent a Roman takeover. Many tribes were won over by political or economic means rather than being subjugated by military force.

Roman Influences

It is not certain when Roman influence in Britain began. The expeditions of Julius Caesar in 55–54 BC were of no great consequence, but contact with the continent had been commonplace long before this. The people of Britain were closely related to their continental cousins, and had contact with Rome through them before the Roman conquest of Britain began.

Over the next decades, the Roman Empire planned invasions and made agreements with various tribes that brought them into client status with the empire, and finally invaded as a result of a chaotic political situation in Britain. Disputes between tribes created an opportunity to annex the British Isles, and in 43 AD a

Roman force landed in Britain. Despite initial resistance, Rome conquered southern Britain and gradually pushed its frontiers north and west.

There was no concept of Britain as a nation at this time, or for several centuries afterwards. Britain was a place in which numerous tribes had their territory; it was tribal loyalties that predominated rather than any concept of realms or regions. This tribalism persisted under Roman rule, but was eroded to some extent as the Britons became Romanized.

THERE WAS NO CONCEPT OF A BRITISH NATION IN THIS ERA; TRIBAL LOYALTIES PREDOMINATED.

Roman-controlled Britain was a province of the empire until around 410 AD, when Roman troops were withdrawn to defend territories closer to home. Parts of the British Isles lay outside Roman control of course; the tribes of Caledonia (Scotland) successfully resisted Roman incursions for the most part, and Hibernia (Ireland) was completely beyond the control of Rome.

At the time of the Roman invasion, the role of cavalry was fulfilled among the Britons by chariots. This practice was outdated elsewhere, but had been retained in the British Isles and was used with some success. With Romanization came the use of cavalry; in 175 a force of Sarmatian horsemen was deployed in Britain. Sarmatia lay north of the Black Sea, roughly where the modern nation of Ukraine is found today.

LEFT: Although the chariot was obsolete in Continental Europe, the Ancient Britons made effective use of its mobility. Chariot forces essentially combined the mobility of cavalry with the ability to jump down and fight on foot, then return to the chariot and escape from a bad situation.

Sarmatians at War

This force of cavalry was sent to Britain as a result of a peace treaty after a war between the Roman Empire and the Sarmatians. Part of the settlement was an agreement to provide troops, the majority of whom were sent to Britain. The initial deployment was 5500 men, which was a very significant force in that era. It is known that much, but not all, of the force was withdrawn in later years.

The Sarmatian cavalry force was given a settlement at what is today Ribchester, in Lancashire, where veterans settled down. As well as their military contribution, these mounted warriors brought with them traditions and myths. Among them were tales

BELOW: The Romans were great organizers. Their fort at Ribchester followed a standard pattern, combining good defences with efficient logistics. Like many similar forts, it became the focus for a community of retired soldiers who settled in the surrounding area.

of a king whose band of mounted warriors possessed a magical cup that only the best of them were permitted to drink from. This device, the Nartyamonga, bears a distinct resemblance to the Holy Grail of the Arthurian legends.

There are other similarities between the Arthur of Britain and the hero Batraz in the Sarmatians' mythology. Arthur's dying wish that his sword be cast into the lake closely parallels a Sarmatian tradition, and in some Medieval depictions Arthur fights under a banner that resembles a traditional Sarmatian war banner. Interestingly, a similar set of tales existed in what is now France, probably as a result of Alan tribesmen settling there around 375 AD. However, Lancelot supplants Arthur in the lead role in many of these tales.

One possible 'proto-Arthur' is a Roman soldier named Lucius Artorius Castus. Late in his career, around 181 AD, Artorius was placed in command of Sarmatian cavalry who were serving as auxiliaries to the Roman occupation forces. This force served against invading Caledonian tribesmen, and acted as a 'fire brigade' rapid response force to deal with other troubles. It was also deployed to Armorica in northern Gaul to deal with an insurrection there. It is possible that these fast-moving armoured cavalrymen made such an impression that distorted tales of their exploits were remembered centuries afterwards.

ABOVE: **After his service in Britain, Lucius Artorius Castus was granted high office in Liburnia, in modern-day Croatia, where he died. Local monuments commemorate the King Arthur connection, which has the support of a number of historians.**

Among the connections made from this version of events is the idea of a dragon banner being the symbol of these warriors. This would explain the name 'Pendragon' associated with Arthur, but there is no real evidence either way. Indeed, there is little historical evidence to indicate that Artorius was anything like as important as this legend suggests. The man himself did live and was for a time governor of a Roman province – albeit one far from Britain – but he is not recorded as having carried out heroic exploits at the head of his cavalry.

Whether or not Artorius was a proto-Arthur, the legends of the Sarmatian cavalrymen he was associated with have several similarities with the Arthur story. Their heroes mostly fought earthly foes but were also opposed by supernatural creatures. Batraz, a hero of the Sarmatian legends, gained his magic sword by pulling it from the roots of a tree, and upon his death asked a friend to hurl it into the sea. Just as in the Arthurian cycle, his friend did not wish to do so but eventually complied.

LEFT: **Sarmatian cavalrymen, as depicted on Trajan's Column (second century AD), shows them in their characteristic scale armour. It was composed of small, overlapping metal scales fixed to a thick backing and offered good protection against most weapons.**

ARMOURED WARRIORS

The Sarmatian cavalry may have included lightly armoured horse archers and light cavalry equipped with lances, but the main striking force was heavy cavalry, or 'cataphracts'. These were protected by scale armour, formed from many small metal plates (scales) attached to a backing material such as leather and possibly overlapped to prevent gaps. Horses were similarly armoured. Scale armour offered excellent protection but was heavy and less flexible than chain mail. However, this did not prevent cataphracts from using their weapons effectively.

The Sarmatian cataphracts in Roman service were armed with a lance as their primary weapon on horseback, backed up by a sword and a dagger. A composite bow was also carried, enabling the cavalry to soften up their opponents with archery before charging home with the lance and sword. These very potent and versatile mounted warriors were no doubt a fearsome force on the battlefield, and as the original Sarmatian members of the force retired or went home, locals would be recruited to replace them.

It is possible that this 'Sarmatian' force was still in existence when Roman troops were withdrawn from Britain. If so, their traditions would have been maintained along with their arms, equipment and fighting style. Sarmatian myths such as that of Batraz and his sword would have been passed on and absorbed into local culture, adding to Celtic and Roman mythology. Another possibility for the 'real Arthur' is a leader of whatever remained of these post-Sarmatian cataphracts after the Roman withdrawal.

The Coming of the Saxons

By the time Roman forces left Britain, around 410 AD, pressure was already mounting from Saxon raiding parties. These were initially prevented from settling by Roman and Romano-British forces, but by 450 AD or so it was no longer possible to prevent Saxons from gaining control of parts of Southeast England. This date is known as the *Adventus Saxonum*, or the 'Coming of the English' – Saxon in this case usually translates as 'English'.

Once established, the new territories expanded due to the arrival of more Anglo-Saxons and the conquest of new territories accompanied by the absorption of the populations dwelling there. Historians are divided as to whether there was a large-scale migration of Anglo-Saxons into Britain or a more gradual drift of smaller numbers, but certainly the area controlled by the Saxons and the number of warriors they could field increased over time.

The misconception that this was a 'Dark Age' in which civilization collapsed and everyone lived in violent misery is less prevalent than it used to be. Indeed, it is arguable that one reason why Britain was poorly equipped to resist these Saxon incursions

BELOW: The 'Saxons' who invaded Britain were actually several Germanic peoples, including Angles, Saxons and Jutes. Their customs and dress were sufficiently similar that they were generally perceived as a single group by the Britons.

is that it had become relatively peaceful and civilized during its time as a Roman province. St Gildas, writing in the sixth century AD, blamed the Saxon conquest of Britain largely on the 'luxuria' and self-indulgence of the upper echelons of British society.

According to St Gildas and other sources, the Saxons agreed to act as *foederati* – a Roman concept, which essentially meant barbarian people from outside the empire defending its frontiers in return for payment – protecting the Britons from Caledonian incursions. This arrangement collapsed and resulted in a Saxon rampage across Britain, followed by new treaties. Saxon influence continued to grow, however, and further conflict was perhaps inevitable.

The people referred to as Saxons or Anglo-Saxons were, in fact, of varied origin. Most were originally Germanic, but the term 'Saxon' later came to refer to anyone from the Saxon-controlled regions of Britain and probably included large numbers of native Britons. By the end of the fifth century AD, these Saxons were well rooted in Britain and could be considered native, although they were joined by others coming from overseas.

THE SAXONS REPLACED THE CALEDONIANS AS THE GREATEST THREAT TO THE ANCIENT BRITONS.

It is notable that Roman military equipment was still in use in Britain at this time, and was issued to Saxon warriors serving as foederati. However, over time the influence of Rome gradually faded and was replaced by an emerging British culture combining Romano-British influences with older Celtic concepts and ideas brought by Saxon invaders from the continent.

The invaders also brought with them their language. Latin scholarship had not died out in Britain when the legions went home, but the dominant language was Brythonic. This was of Celtic origin and was spoken throughout most of Britain; in what is now Scotland the (probably related) Pictish language was more common. Brythonic was gradually replaced by the language of the Anglo-Saxons, becoming what is now known as Old English. The Brythonic languages survived in regions such as Brittany, Wales and Cornwall.

An Early Arthur?

Some early tales of King Arthur have him defending Britain against Saxon invaders in the late fifth or early sixth century. There was no armour of steel plate at this time; Arthur's warriors would have looked nothing like the mounted knights of most movie depictions. It is quite likely that equipment left over from the Romano-British era was long gone and that this Arthur and his men fought on foot even if they had horses for mobility.

If this was the case, they would have been armed with well-made swords, spears and axes that might have been a long-handled, two-handed version. Armour would be chain mail or small metal plates fixed to a padded or leather backing. Some men might even have had old Roman equipment – armour and weapons lasted a long time if well cared for.

Nor would these warriors have followed any sort of 'code of chivalry'. That would not be created for several centuries, along with jousting and knightly tournaments. They would have been close companions of their lord, likely friends and family as well as followers, and would constitute an élite fighting force, not least because they were used to working as a team.

These early Brythonic warriors could perhaps be mistaken for a bunch of scruffy barbarians by someone expecting knightly manners and heraldry, but they were the defenders of an advanced and complex culture. They might not have been literate, but scholarship had not died out when the so-called 'Dark Ages' began. Perhaps more mundane than mythical, these men would nonetheless have been heroes and staunch defenders of their people.

Warfare in this era was on a smaller scale than had been the case during the Roman age. Most conflicts involved what were essentially quite small skirmishes between warbands rather than armies. Individual prowess and inspiring leadership could be a decisive factor, as could the teamwork of a band used to working together.

It has been suggested that for some reason the warriors of this 'Dark Age' were ignorant buffoons who hacked mindlessly at one another until someone was injured more or less at random.

BELOW: The warriors of post-Roman Britain would not have resembled Medieval knights in any way. They were Celtic tribesmen who wore colourful clothing and fought with well-made iron weapons in the manner of the Gauls who opposed Julius Caesar centuries earlier.

ABOVE: **Typical weapons of the Brythonic tribesman were a spear and a shield with a metal boss. A wealthy man might be able to afford a sword, which would be well made and skilfully handled.**

Similarly, there exists a common misconception that weapons were large and clumsy, contributing to the general ineptitude of warriors. In truth, some elements of the military art did fall into disuse and were possibly forgotten about, but skill at arms remained highly important.

The weaponry wielded by these Brythonic warriors would be at least competently made, and might be excellent in the case of a rich warrior who could afford the finest of swords. It was also wielded with skill, at least in the case of experienced warriors or those whose business was war. Gone were the days of complex military training such as that received by Roman legionnaires, but skill at arms was still passed on.

IN SINGLE COMBAT, THE WARRIORS OF SIXTH CENTURY BRITAIN WERE A MATCH FOR ANYONE.

The average farmer who turned out to fight with his spear might not have much idea of how to use it – beyond the obvious – and would have been easy prey for a skilled and trained warrior. Those warriors did exist, making up the core of a fighting force based around the chief's warband, and they would have been as effective as any other warriors from any period of history, at least on a small-force basis. A properly handled professional army might defeat such a force without undue difficulty, but man for man the warriors of the fifth and sixth century were a match for anyone.

They were, apparently, a match for the Saxons. The Britons were gradually pushed back, not so much because they were outfought by the invaders, but because they were defeated piecemeal. Had the Britons united to resist the invaders, the situation might have been quite different. However, they did not and Saxon control increased. By 500 AD, the situation for the Britons was desperate and they were forced to present a unified front. According to legend, their resurgence was led by King Arthur.

The Battle of Badon Hill

There is no historical evidence for Arthur leading the united Britons, although there are records of an individual named Ambrosius Aurelianus. Aurelianus seems to have been a Romano-Briton of noble family, who was probably a Christian. Under his leadership – or possibly that of his successors – the Britons managed to defeat the invaders in a series of major battles. The greatest of these was the Battle of Badon Hill.

The location and exact date of this battle are not known. Among the possible locations are Somerset, Wiltshire, southern Scotland and various points in Southeast England. The legendary version of the battle has Arthur slaying 940 Saxons by his own

BELOW: The Battle of Badon Hill has been depicted in various different ways. Very little is known about what actually happened, and what records exist are not reliable. It seems rather unlikely that one man slew nearly a thousand Saxons all by himself.

hand, although God Almighty is also given a share of the credit for this achievement. This defeat was so overwhelming that Saxon incursions were halted for almost 50 years.

Despite the efforts of these Brythonic warriors, Saxon expansion continued and eventually Britain was overrun. In 577 AD the Saxon King of Wessex defeated Brythonic forces and gained control over modern-day Gloucestershire, Somerset and Oxfordshire. Another decisive defeat in 615 AD drove the remaining Britons to the continent – mainly Brittany – and to Scotland, Wales and Cornwall. Most of Britain was now dominated by Anglo-Saxon culture.

BY THE EARLY 600s, MOST OF MAINLAND BRITAIN WAS UNDER SAXON CONTROL.

It is worth noting that the Arthur depicted in this version of events spoke a language that was displaced by what became Old English and belonged to a culture that was supplanted in most of Britain. The rise of Saxon dominance did not, however, unify the British Isles nor create a single nation out of their people. In that, nothing had changed – there was still no nation of Britain or England, so while someone might be called 'King of the Britons', there was no such thing as a King of Britain. Instead, several small kingdoms arose and at times warred with one another.

BELOW: By the late 700s, Norse traders had begun to arrive in England. Soon afterwards the notorious Viking raids began. These increased in scale over the next two centuries, from single ships to huge fleets carrying thousands of warriors.

Early Kingdoms of England

The Saxon kingdoms of England gradually changed in character into something recognizably early English. The Germanic paganism of the invaders was supplanted by Christianity, but this did not happen overnight.

Christianity had probably arrived in Britain in the first century AD by way of the Roman occupation. Initially, few Britons became Christians, but over time the new religion gained adherents. It is likely that most of Britain was at least notionally Christian by the time Rome withdrew. However, Christianity was largely replaced by the Germanic religion of the Saxon invaders until rekindled from 600 AD onwards. Thereafter Christianity once more became the dominant religion in Britain, with great cathedrals such as those at Canterbury and York built in the 700s.

These early English kingdoms were challenged by raids from the Norsemen – so-called Vikings – from 793 AD onwards and resisted with varying degrees of success. Raids were followed by small-scale settlement and then by an attempt at conquest. By 875 AD the only Saxon kingdom remaining in England was Wessex. Despite setbacks Alfred, King of Wessex (r. 871–899), was able to mount an effective resistance and prevent a Norse takeover of Britain. However, the Norsemen were now part of the British political landscape and had their own kingdoms in the British Isles.

King Alfred gained the epithet 'The Great' for his defence of his homeland against the invaders, but does not seem to have ever been considered as a candidate for a proto-Arthur. His tale does parallel some of the key elements of the Arthurian legends, however, and may have influenced later storytellers to incorporate some aspects of his story into that of Arthur. He did not defeat the Norse invaders in his own lifetime, but his grandson Eadred (920–955 AD) ruled a united England.

This unity was at times very shaky, and was challenged by further Norse incursions. The Norsemen, like the Britons and Saxons, mostly fought on foot although they were happy enough to use horses for mobility. However, Norse society was also evolving and ultimately created the next set of invaders: the Normans. The Normans were, in fact, Norsemen who had been given land on the northern coast of what is now France in return for defending it. In this, the Frankish king essentially made the Norsemen into a new form of *foederati*, and over time the Frankish and Norman cultures blended. Many 'Normans' were not of Norse descent, they were Franks who now lived under the rule of the new Norman society and were adopted into it.

BELOW: Although Alfred the Great led a successful defence of Britain from the invading Norsemen, he does not seem to be a candidate for a 'real King Arthur'. However, he did lay the groundwork for a unified kingdom of England.

Norman Knights Conquer England

In 1066 the King of England died, leaving three claimants to the throne. One was Harold Godwinson, who defeated the Norseman Harald Hardrada in the north of England to secure his throne but was then forced to march rapidly south to meet the third contender for the crown – Duke William of Normandy.

The army under Harold was typically English in character, created by influences going back 1000 years and more to Celtic warfare before the Roman invasion. It was also influenced by the Norse style of combat, and was characterized by a defensive shieldwall tactic. Some men carried bows, but most were armed with spears. Elite housecarls – personal retainers of the nobility and professional fighting men – were armed with long-handled axes and swords.

BELOW: **Harold's infantry-based English army was defeated at Hastings by a combination of Norman archery, infantry and cavalry attacks. The Norman Conquest ushered in a new era in Britain, in which the armoured horseman was the primary force on the battlefield.**

Opposing them, the Normans had adopted cavalry as their main striking arm. By the time of the Norman invasion, the elite of the army was mounted, armed with lance and sword and armoured in chain mail. These men are normally called knights nowadays, but the word 'knight' actually originates from the Saxon 'cniht', a word meaning the personal retainer of a noblemen. Since these were fighting men in service to a lord, the term is entirely applicable to the Norman heavy cavalry, but they would not have considered themselves knights as such – and nor would they know anything about a code of chivalry.

The Norman conquest of Britain brought with it linguistic changes that created Middle English and a new social order in which the Norman military class were rulers. It also marked the return of armoured cavalry as the pre-eminent military arm in Britain, and thus the beginnings of the 'era of the knight' that is generally depicted in Arthurian fiction.

Armoured horsemen were not the only type of soldier fielded, of course, but they were the main striking arm and the force capable of the fastest engagement. A handful of heavy cavalrymen, or even a lone armoured horseman, was still a formidable concentration of military power, and, of course, the members of this elite were also the ruling class.

Norman Fortifications

The Normans built great cathedrals, partly for religious reasons and partly as a means of social control. The presence of a huge, impressive building on the skyline was a reminder of the superiority of the ruling class that helped keep the peasantry in line. They also constructed a great many fortifications. These were initially rather basic 'motte and bailey' type forts, with a main defensive structure on a mound (motte) surrounded by a ditch, and an outer area (bailey) protected by a wooden palisade and another ditch.

Forts of this kind were limited in how much protection they offered, but they were a vast improvement on nothing at all. A fort provided the troops stationed there with a secure base where they could rest and store provisions, and where they were less

ABOVE: **Early Norman fortifications were simple constructions of wood and earth, but soon stone castles began to be built and were extended over time. Thus impressive castles such as Alnwick in Northumberland represent the final form of the structure rather than how it would have looked in 1100 AD.**

vulnerable to surprise attack. A handful of chain mail-armoured knights on horseback was a potent military force in the Norman era, but if they could be ambushed while in camp at night they were as vulnerable as any other small group of people. A fort made this sort of surprise attack much less likely.

A HANDFUL OF ARMOURED HORSEMEN REPRESENTED A POWERFUL FORCE IN THE NORMAN ERA.

Fortifications of this sort were more than a physical barrier to attack. They were also a psychological deterrent. Not only was a fortification a reminder of the power of the owners, but it also made it virtually impossible for a sudden attack or rebellion to overwhelm the local lord. Reduced chances of success were a deterrent to potential attackers or rebels, and so the forts contributed to security in less obvious ways.

These early fortifications were no more impressive than the local population could build; Saxon burghs were often surrounded by a ditch and rampart with a wooden palisade on top. However,

RIGHT: Much of what is known about the Battle of Hastings and the surrounding events is inferred from the Bayeux Tapestry. Opinions are divided about the meaning of some elements, such as the exact design of armour and the use of the lance.

as the new Norman overlords consolidated their hold on Britain, they began to replace wooden forts with stone castles. Stone walls around towns also began to appear. There was nothing new about building fortifications from stone, but the amount of work involved was often beyond the capability of Saxon communities.

The fact that the Normans could muster the manpower and organize the task was another demonstration of their power. The new stone fortifications were an even stronger symbol of the overlords' control. The castle building art advanced, not least to keep pace with new techniques for assaulting or besieging storing places. Although many castles did not match the Hollywood image of enormous fortifications with grand open spaces inside their walls, some very impressive structures were built during this time.

Knights in Shining Armour?

The earliest fighting men recognizable as 'armoured knights' to appear in Britain were Norman cavalrymen, arriving as already noted in 1066 AD – five centuries after the most likely

'real Arthur' lived. The Norman heavy cavalryman fought on horseback whenever possible, using a lance and shield. His sword was a backup weapon and was effective against unarmoured opponents, but less useful against an equivalently armoured warrior. The cavalry were supported by foot soldiers and archers.

THE PRIMARY WEAPON OF THE NORMAN CAVALRYMAN WAS HIS LANCE, WITH THE SWORD AS A BACKUP.

Chain mail had for many years been the standard form of protection for a well armoured warrior, usually paired with a helm whose design changed through the centuries. Chain mail offered good protection from most weapons, but was heavy and – more importantly – distributed its weight poorly. Most of the weight of armour fell on the user's shoulders and waist, where it was gathered in by a belt.

BELOW: Chain mail offered good protection against most weapons, but its weight was distributed poorly. This was less of a problem for a mounted warrior than for a foot soldier.

Chain mail offered good protection from penetration and spread out the impact of a weapon so that it was easier to absorb, but it did not grant the wearer complete invulnerability. Even a non-penetrating blow could break bones or cause trauma that would take the warrior out of a fight. A padded undergarment reduced the amount of harm a mailed warrior suffered, and offered reasonable protection in its own right. This garment, known as a gambeson, was also worn by troops who had no other protection.

Coat of Arms

The desire to have better protection led to many innovations. Among them was the 'coat of plates' which took the form of metal plates attached to a surcoat. The latter was a garment worn over armour, adopted during the twelfth century. Designs varied, as did colours. White was popular with crusaders as it helped reduce the heating of

PLATE ARMOUR

Plate armour offered increased protection and also better weight distribution. At first, during the late thirteenth century, plates were added to some areas of the body and were worn over chain mail. Articulated plates, with mail used where plates could not offer good protection, gradually supplanted this reinforced chain mail. However, it was not until the early 1400s that full suits of plate armour became available.

Plate distributed weight better than chain, and offered better protection for the same weight of armour. By the fifteenth century, plate was sufficiently common that men-at-arms who were not knights (i.e. they were equipped much the same but did not have a noble title or holdings) could be deployed in significant numbers. Plate armoured warriors were more or less invulnerable to most weapons unless prevented from moving somehow, for example by being wrestled to the ground and then pounded once they were immobile. Wrestling in armour therefore became an essential part of a knight's training – partly to put other knights where they could be effectively attacked and partly to prevent being held immobile and stabbed through the armour joints by a mob of rowdy peasants.

RIGHT: **Plate armour became increasingly sophisticated, offering excellent protection without compromising mobility – though it was, of course, heavy and tiring to wear.**

armour caused by the sun. Once it became popular to display a knight's 'arms' (essentially his insignia), the surcoat was an obvious place – hence the term 'coat of arms'.

The coat of plates was an added layer of protection, which also increased the weight of armour worn by a knight. At no point did warriors become so overburdened by armour that they had to be winched onto their horses – that is pure invention – but the added weight was tiring and could cause problems for a knight who fell surrounded by his enemies.

Protection of this sort made it possible for knights to engage in jousting tournaments without severe risk. That is not to

ABOVE: **King Henri II of France died as a result of a lance splinter entering through a helmet visor that was jammed slightly open. The dying Henri generously forgave his opponent, Count Gabriel of Montgomery, but Montgomery nevertheless considered himself disgraced.**

say there were no accidents – a French king died as a result of a jousting accident despite having the very best equipment available. However, the use of supplementary armour plates – which would be too heavy for use in battle – enabled jousting to take place in relative safety. Specialized tournament armour was also created for fighting on foot.

To counter this heavy armour protection, the Late Medieval knight had access to a range of weapons. His sword was very much a sidearm – better than nothing, but virtually useless against an armoured opponent. It would serve very well against lesser opponents however. To deal with other knights required a specialized armour-piercing weapon such as a war hammer or war pick, or a heavy implement such as an axe or mace. The couched lance (one held firmly under the arm and supported by a suitable saddle) driven home at the charge was also effective.

Improvements in armour and weapons were accompanied by advances in head protection. The Norman knight of 1066 wore an open-faced helm with a nasal bar. Over time this evolved into the great helm, which covered the entire head and offered better protection at the price of reducing vision and ventilation. The great helm was often worn with a chain mail coif or padded hood under it, and to this was sometimes added a smaller metal helmet that fitted inside the great helm.

This under-helm gradually evolved into a form of head protection called a bascinet, which supplanted the great helm. From the early 1300s, hinged visors became available, allowing a knight to open his helm and improve both vision and ventilation. The practice of raising a visor as one approached a superior – to allow the knight to be identified and reduce the chances of treachery – survives today in the form of the military salute.

The bascinet continued to evolve, gaining and losing accessories such as the aventail – a curtain of chain mail hanging from the helm to protect the neck and shoulders – until a great

BELOW: The swordsmanship of the Middle Ages was very sophisticated, with advanced techniques for using the one-handed and two-handed sword. A properly trained swordsman had a huge advantage over someone who only knew how to make the most basic 'peasant's strokes'.

TYPES OF SWORDS

The sword carried by a knight was known as an arming sword, and was designed to be used for cutting strokes delivered with one hand. It was of a fairly simple cruciform shape, with quillons (a crossguard) to protect the user's hand and a counterweighted pommel. Knightly swords were not especially heavy, and the 'felt weight' was relatively slight if the weapon was well balanced. The arming sword was a symbol of status as well as a weapon and was worn under most circumstances, even out of harness (armour).

The longsword was a heavier weapon, although it often had a blade the same length as a typical arming sword. The primary difference was a longer handle to allow the weapon to be used in both hands. This results in references to the arming sword as the 'short sword' which can be misleading'; an arming sword typically had a 70–80cm (28–31in) blade.

The bastard, or hand-and-a-half, sword was also a heavier weapon designed to be used with one or both hands. Improved armour protection meant that a shield was no longer as necessary as it had been in the past, allowing the knight to carry a more powerful two-handed weapon that gave him more options and a better chance of penetrating an opponent's armour. The estoc, or tuck, was a purely thrusting sword intended for use against heavy armour.

many varieties of helm existed. Some had a very pointed snout, to deflect lance blows coming straight in at the face, while others had a flatter design. By around 1450 the bascinet in all its forms was falling out of use in favour of the armet and sallet. These helms were extremely strong and well shaped to deflect blows of all kinds. By this time fluted 'gothic armour' was available. Many generic depictions of 'knights in armour' or Arthur's knights show them in this fully articulated place armour with a sallet, even though it was only in use during the Late Medieval era.

The Late Medieval Era

The Renaissance is generally considered to have begun in 1450 or so, although it did not really reach Britain until the reign of Elizabeth I (1533–1603). Thus the first flowerings of the Renaissance were taking place in some regions at a time when the British Isles were still in the throes of the Wars of the Roses – very much a Medieval conflict. Renaissance warfare is generally associated with an increasing use of firearms, but these were available much earlier.

Cannon had been in use against fortifications for some time when they first made an appearance on the field of battle. This was at Crecy in 1346. Early cannon were large and clumsy, suited only to static defence or battering at fortifications. Similarly, hand-gonnes (or hand cannon) were in use in the 1300s, but were limited in their effectiveness. Two men were required to aim and fire a hand-gonne, which was little more than a metal pot on a stick, with a ball propelled more or less at random out of it by exploding gunpowder.

Although not very effective, these weapons were in use, especially in siege warfare, during the era depicted in many versions of the Arthurian legend. Indeed, in at least one version Mordred's cannon can be heard firing in the distance as Arthur meets with his knights for the last time before the fatal battle at Camlann.

BELOW: **The Bascinet helm evolved into many variations. The pointed visor/face plate and sloped design helped deflect the force of a blow, a vital consideration in an era where a knight might receive a lance thrust to the face.**

There was no standing army in this era. Powerful lords maintained a personal force of cavalry and foot soldiers, and brought this with them when they came to fight for their superiors. This feudal military system was based upon a set of responsibilities and duties, with each social stratum able to command some members of the one immediately below it and through them the next strata. Chains of loyalty and duty ran from the lowest levels right up to the king, but were subject to limits. A lord could only command his vassals to provide so many days' military service per year, and even the king could ask only so much.

This system was efficient in that it enabled a fighting force to be assembled at need, but dispersed when not required. A system evolved whereby settlements were ruled by members of the upper class who created a military ruling elite. Law and judgement were provided by these lords of the manor, and if the law required enforcement the lord rode out personally to see to it – at least in theory. A small settlement could support one nobleman who might employ a handful of less well equipped fighting men to defend his person and property, and would accompany him when he went to join a larger force created by his liege lord.

The feudal system essentially placed a small fighting force in each settlement to dispense and uphold law, and not coincidentally put fighting men where they could be supported by produce from the settlement and its surrounding farms. This was little different from the Anglo-Saxon system, whereby fighting men were also supported from land farmed by the local settlement. It was cost effective in many ways, but had significant drawbacks.

Among these was the difficulty in supporting a large-scale military campaign that would take men away from their farms

ABOVE: The hand-gonne was an extremely primitive and unreliable weapon whose effect on the battlefield was probably minimal. However, it made a suitably impressive amount of noise and smoke, and may have been demoralizing to those under its fire.

and estates for an extended period. There was no formal logistics system in place, and although supplies were provided an army was expected to forage while on campaign. In enemy territory this was combined with deliberate destruction to attack the enemy economy and could be an effective means of waging war, but it also meant that an army was vulnerable to running out of food.

Shifting Balance of Power

Another drawback of the feudal system, although one that had important consequences for the freedom and protection of the non-noble classes, was the gradual shift in power from the king to the nobility. In the early Middle Ages a king had absolute authority and could command the great lords without fear of consequences, but as time passed and their power grew the lords became able to resist royal commands. A form of political bargaining became necessary in which the king was still officially an absolute monarch, but he had to tread more carefully when dealing with his great nobility.

One result of this move away from absolute royal power was the Magna Carta of 1215, which granted rights to the lower

BELOW: The Magna Carta represented a change in attitudes to kingship. No longer was the king above the law, but was now bound by limitations on his power. Non-nobles also received a measure of legal protection that had not previously existed.

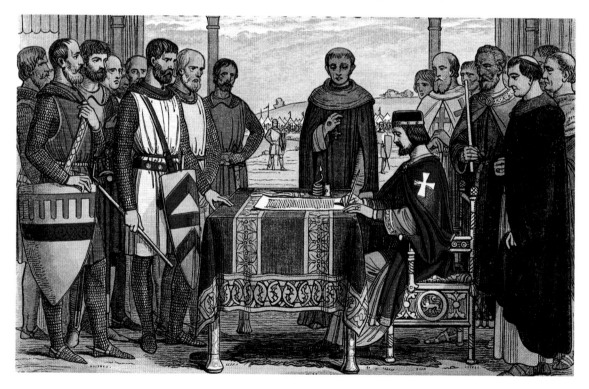

classes and established that the king was no longer above the law. This was an important change in society and reflected a situation in which the king had to ask for the support of his great nobility for major undertakings such as a foreign war, and could be threatened by a powerful lord in a manner that would not have been possible a century earlier.

Foreign wars were, of course, undertaken. Wars were fought to subdue Wales, and against Scotland and France. Most notable of these was the Hundred Years War, which was more properly a series of related conflicts running from 1337 to 1453. The sort of arms and equipment often depicted in movie versions of the Arthurian legends – and, indeed, most visual media set in the Middle Ages – tend to be from this era.

THE ARMS AND ARMOUR DEPICTED IN MOST MOVIES DATE FROM THE LATE MIDDLE AGES.

Waging War

Warfare in the late Middle Ages generally involved few large-scale field battles. Sieges and the capture of strong places, such as cities and important castles were far more important, with battles often fought to break a siege or prevent an army from beginning one. Raids in force, devastating the countryside to weaken the enemy economy, were also common and, again, could result in a battle. However, battles were not fought for the sake of it.

There is a common misconception that Medieval warfare consisted mainly of grubby peasants sent forward to ineptly stab at one another with inadequate weapons, followed by a reckless charge by the knights – often through their own infantry. There is a grain of truth in this, but, in fact, Medieval commanders were good strategists and fought for solid reasons, such as political or economic advantage. The martial culture of the time was such that the knightly cavalry could be impetuous, but warfare was generally more sophisticated than might commonly be imagined.

Some versions of the Arthur story are set in the High to Late Middle Ages, in which case the armoured knight would still be the elite of the army, but was backed up by other troops including professional infantry and light cavalry. English forces would make extensive use of the longbow, while bows, crossbows and even slings might be in use in other regions. Cannon might be present on the battlefield, and would certainly be in use during a siege.

These elements are often quietly forgotten about in dramatized versions of the Arthurian legends, presumably because they could detract from the heroic actions of plate-armoured knights or confuse an audience who might not know that gunpowder existed alongside the lance and knightly sword. An Arthur story with knights in full plate would be anachronistic if it did not reflect the reality of the era in which such armour was available. If cannon and hand-gonnes are not wanted, then the story needs to be set a little earlier, perhaps in the High Middle Ages. This period is considered to be from 1000–1300 AD, and a realistic depiction of the Arthur story would have to show the armour and weapons of the time along with fortifications and construction techniques. Early in this period, a fortification might be of wood and earth rather than the grand stone-built castles commonly associated with King Arthur and his knights. More importantly perhaps, the code of chivalry that underpins much of the Arthurian legend did not exist.

ABOVE: One of the most potent forces on the battlefield was the English longbowman, who was a free commoner.

Chivalry, Heraldry and the Tournament

The term 'chivalry' has come to be associated with good manners, protection of the weak, respect for women and so forth, but actually had very different origins. It derives from the French 'chevalrie', and basically referred to ownership of a horse. To be able to afford the arms and equipment of a horsed warrior meant being a member of the upper strata of society, but this did not say anything about the horseman's character.

However, before the creation of a code of chivalry there was a general expectation about the conduct of a noble-born fighting man. He was expected to be skilled at arms and courageous, of course, and also loyal. There was an expectation of generosity and hospitality to those of appropriate social class, and a lack of greed. The latter had various connotations, not least that a warrior should be above taking bribes to betray his liege lord or his fellows, and also that he would not manipulate a situation for his own gain. This essentially boils down to the expectation that a fighting man should be willing and able to do his job despite risks, and should be trustworthy.

A MAN-AT-ARMS WAS EXPECTED TO BE COURAGEOUS, LOYAL AND MERCIFUL.

In some cases there was also a belief that the strong should protect the weak and show mercy when possible. This was often patchily applied; even after the code of chivalry had been well established it was not uncommon for knights to protect the virtue only of noble women while doing whatever they pleased to the common peasantry. Warriors were also expected to control their temper, at least at court or in the presence of the great nobility, and thus avoid pointless disputes and fights that might lead to a feud.

The concept of honour encapsulated most of this behaviour, and in this context it can be seen as more than just a high ideal – it was a way of ensuring that the warrior class was reliable and not riven by mistrust and enmity. This pre-chivalric code served the ends of the king by creating a situation where a warrior who put his own gain first or failed to live up to the expected standards of bravery would be disgraced. Lacking honour was ruinous in such a society, so the concept acted as a social regulator.

Courtly Love

Between 1170 and 1220, this unspoken code of conduct was gradually formalized into the code of chivalry to which all nobles were expected to aspire. Chivalric behaviour varied somewhat from one region to another, but generally there was an expectation of piety, duty and honour. Other social customs crept into the general concept of chivalry, such as courtly love.

Courtly love varied over time and between regions. It might be nothing more than a fashionable affectation, whereby knights would extravagantly declare their love for a lady and perhaps wear her colours to show their devotion. This might or might not be accompanied by real affection; in some cases it was expected of a knight to be in love with an unattainable woman, or to profess love for a noblewoman to show loyalty. The object of affection might or might not be married; courtly love often had nothing to do with physical or emotional attraction.

However, in some cases courtly love was an outlet for real emotions. In an age of arranged marriages that might be entirely loveless, it could be possible for two people to be openly in love without any suggestion of impropriety – although adultery and sexual liaisons between courtly lovers were also possible. It is not clear how much of the concept is pure invention on the part of chroniclers and storytellers, but if it is an invention then it is a persistent one. The idea of courtly love pervades many of the Arthurian legends, but appeared relatively late in the Medieval period – if it appeared at all.

BELOW: This casket depicts scenes of courtly love drawn from Medieval poetry on the subject. Troubadours singing songs and reciting poems, often on the subject of love, were popular at the courts of Europe in the eleventh to fourteenth centuries.

Another relatively late invention was heraldry. The idea of displaying insignia or decoration on shields, banners and clothing predates the Arthurian legends by centuries, but became particularly

important after the great helm came into use. Telling friend from foe in a chaotic mêlée has always been a problem, but for a warrior wearing a helm with only narrow vision slits it was even more difficult.

There are no signs of heraldry in the Bayeux Tapestry, which depicts Norman heavy cavalry at the time of the invasion of England. The earliest known examples of a coat of arms that could be inherited by other members of a family occur in the early 1100s, and initially there were no formal rules about such insignia.

HERALDRY AS WE KNOW IT TODAY DID NOT EXIST AT THE TIME OF THE NORMAN CONQUEST.

Over time, conventions emerged about how coats of arms were combined in the case of marriage, and how they were modified for first, second and subsequent sons. Rules for the use of different colours and the placement of elements in a coat of arms were codified over time, but it was not until the Late Middle Ages (well after 1300) that heraldry achieved the form we now associate with it. An Arthurian knight of 1200 might have some sort of heraldic device on his shield or his surcoat, but the colourful and complex coats of arms often associated with Arthur's knights did not exist in most of the eras in which they are supposed to have lived.

Building a Reputation

Tournaments play a large part in the Arthurian tales, but they, too are a relatively late invention – at least in the form normally depicted. Competitive training had been used by the Romans and possibly earlier civilizations, and it is known that mounted warriors participated in games during the 800s in what is now France. However, there is no indication of the social event or the pageantry associated with the tournament in that era.

The earliest form of tournament in England was a sort of agreed training fight between knights who met up for the purpose at a prearranged spot. It could also be used to settle disputes and establish a pecking order among the nobility. Tournaments of this sort were conducted with real weapons and serious injuries were common. Thus the benefits of extremely realistic training were offset by the loss of skilled fighting men.

Attempts to regulate the bloodshed while maintaining the training value of a 'tourney' led to more formal contests being staged using blunted weapons. Gradually these events took on a greater social importance, and they became pageants that showed off the power and wealth of the tournament's sponsor. They also provided opportunities for competitors to demonstrate their skill and reaffirm their loyalty to their lord. In some areas the social aspect eventually became more important; in others the martial training side was paramount.

Tournaments were a way for a young knight to make a name for himself and perhaps win wealth if prizes were offered. There were also other opportunities. In some areas, a knight might ask to be granted a token of a lady's favour and carry it in the tournament as a declaration of courtly love – which might or might not be accompanied by real romance. In some regions, however, the token was a guarantee of the lady's favours if the bearer did well – it was socially acceptable even for a married woman to give herself to a tournament victor in this manner.

Jousting and Hand-to-Hand Combat

The tournament itself took the form of a parade by the participants followed by various events. Single combat on foot was one, as was jousting on horseback. The joust evolved over time. Initially, it was a single combat that started on horseback with the lance but which might continue with hand weapons on horseback, or with one or both participants on foot if either were unhorsed. This gradually evolved into a form where only lances were used, broken weapons being replaced until one combatant was unhorsed and thereby lost the contest.

Later forms of jousting used lighter lances that broke easily, and were more of a demonstration of skill rather than an attempt to knock the opponent off his horse. Injuries did occur (King Henry II of France was mortally wounded in a jousting accident in 1599) but for the most part these later contests were much safer. The stakes were also different – in early tournaments the losers forfeited their horses and equipment, whereas later the contest was for an agreed prize put up by the organizer. Other demonstrations of skill also took place, such as riding a course while cutting and thrusting at targets with the sword or picking up rings of rope on a lance.

Many tournaments also included a mêlée. This was very common in early events but became less popular over time. Some mêlées were between two sides, others were a free-for-all, although it was not uncommon for groups of knights to team up and use their numbers against the opponents. A strategy of overwhelming one opponent after another could garner a group of knights several very valuable warhorses and sets of armour, thereby vastly increasing their wealth. This may have run contrary to the emerging code of chivalry, but it was an effective way for a skilled knight to go about enriching himself.

The heyday of the tournament was around 1150–1250, after which it declined in popularity, although jousting competitions continued and were often referred to as tournaments. Tournamenting proper was replaced to a great extent by events that served the same social purpose, but dispensed with some or even all of the violence. In the meantime, the *pas d'armes*, which was a sort of unofficial tournament, became popular. A knight or group of knights would position themselves at a bridge

BELOW: The formal joust, with competitors separated by a tilt barrier, was a relatively late invention. The term 'joust' originally meant a 'meeting' between knights and could involve combat with swords and other weapons.

or some other chokepoint and challenge any passing knight to a contest. Social convention required that the knight accept or be disgraced.

The *pas d'armes* features in several of the Arthurian legends. There are numerous occasions where knights randomly camp out at some inconvenient spot and force passers-by to fight them. Some of the characters meet new friends this way; some are slowed in their mission and some have to fight enemies. One aspect of the pas d'armes that might be pure invention was the practice of 'capturing' an item from any noble lady who passed by and symbolically holding it hostage until a knight won the contest and could triumphantly return it. This was another expression of courtly love, and may or may not have ever happened in reality.

Tournaments of a sort were still occurring as late as the reign of King Henry VIII of England (1509–1547). As part of a diplomatic meeting with King Francis I of France at the Field of the Cloth of Gold in 1520 there was an event that was mostly pageant but which did include jousting and other challenges of martial skill. However, the usual depiction of the Late Medieval tournament replete with heraldry and jousting in plate armour is largely anachronistic.

It is obvious, then, that the various traditional elements of the Arthurian tales come from very different times. An Arthur who fights Saxon invaders cannot wear heraldic symbols or plate armour, and would have no idea what a code of chivalry might be. The depiction of Arthur that best fits the Medieval tales might be a Norman-style knight of 1250 or so, but the best historical candidates are from six centuries earlier… and, of course, this does not even consider any supernatural elements.

The most likely explanation is that there never was a King Arthur as depicted in the classic tales, and that he is a composite character based on historical figures from as far afield as Sarmatia and Rome. The Arthur character has been placed into a suitable setting for each tale that the author wanted to tell, with varying degrees of disregard for historical reality.

Any given version of the Arthurian legend tends to emphasize one aspect. Usually this is one of the possible historical figures or the mythical Medieval king, but sometimes it may be a new twist on the traditional character. It is simply not possible to reconcile all of the possible versions of the story with any of the possible 'real Arthurs'. Elements of some tales could not exist in the time where others are set. Some versions are internally inconsistent as well, but this is of concern mainly to historians.

Arguably, the most likely historical 'Arthur' lived in the fifth or sixth century and fought the Saxons. The best approximation of the society depicted in tales of the round table and the Grail quest might be 1250–1300 AD. The heraldry and general appearance of castles and armour as shown in many movies looks like a Late Medieval society dating from 1450 or so. None of these are compatible with the others if historical accuracy is to be maintained.

THE TALE OF KING ARTHUR IS AN ADVENTURE STORY SET AGAINST A PSEUDO-HISTORICAL BACKGROUND.

However, the tale of Arthur and his knights is not a history of Britain. It is an adventure story set against a pseudo-historical backdrop. Most of us care less about accuracy and more about being told a good story with a suitably heroic cast, and in that regard few versions of the Arthurian legend fail to deliver.

2

THE EARLY LEGENDS

The earliest known written references to Arthur as a King of the Britons are in the pseudo-historical *Historia Regum Britanniae* ('History of the Kings of Britain'), written by Galfridus Monemutensis (Geoffrey of Monmouth).

Geoffrey of Monmouth was long assumed to be a Welshman, but it seems more likely that he was descended from Breton stock. If so, his family may have been among the upper echelons of society, and would have migrated to Britain after the Norman Conquest.

Given the name by which he refers to himself, Geoffrey of Monmouth was presumably born in or near Monmouth, a town lying just on the Welsh side of the border with England. It was a Norman possession from the 1070s or 1080s, so by the time Geoffrey wrote his pseudo-history around 1136 there had been plenty of time for local legends to become known to the new arrivals from the continent.

OPPOSITE: **Arthur's magical sword Excalibur, which had magical properties, is an integral part of his myth. Yet Excalibur does not appear in the early tales. Instead, Arthur is armed with a weapon named Caliburn, which is replaced by Excalibur in the later stories.**

BELOW: **A carving of Geoffrey of Monmouth, depicting him as a studious and priestly figure. This image is probably correct – he ended his days as a bishop, though he became a priest quite late in his career.**

Geoffrey of Monmouth probably wrote his works outside Wales, more than likely in Oxford where he was a secular canon of the church of St George. Interestingly, he is sometimes referred to as Geoffrey Arthur in documents relating to his time there. Geoffrey was apparently at the college of St George between 1129 and 1151. In 1152, he was ordained as a priest and within days was named as Bishop of St Asaph in Wales. It is not clear whether he took up his duties there, however; he died in 1054 or 1055.

Norman Invasion

At the time when Geoffrey of Monmouth was writing his chronicles, recent events will have provided a great deal of fodder for his imagination. The Norman conquest of England was followed by a push into Wales. This was not initially planned, but became necessary due to pressure from the Welsh. At the time of the Norman invasion of England, Wales was more or less unified under a single king. This came about during the reign of Gruffydd ap Llywelyn, who died in 1063.

The unified Welsh had clashed with the English before the Normans arrived, but the death of Gruffydd ap Llywelyn caused Wales to fragment back into separate kingdoms. Friction and, not infrequently, fighting between the Welsh and the new Norman regime in England prompted an attempt to pacify Wales. The first phase (1067–81) was not conducted with great determination, but over the next 13 years most of Wales was brought under Norman control.

Wales reasserted its independence around 1101 and more or less drove out the Normans, resulting in further Norman campaigns that were limited in their achievements. The death of Henry I of England in 1135 enabled Stephen of Blois, grandson of William the Conqueror, to seize the throne. This would lead to further conflict in Wales as well as a civil war with Empress Matilda, daughter of Henry I. These events were just beginning to unfold as Geoffrey wrote his pseudo-history.

It would seem that Geoffrey of Monmouth drew heavily upon a document named *Historia Brittonum* that was written in the early 800s.

HISTORIA REGUM BRITANNIAE

In the dedication of his History of the Kings of Britain, Geoffrey of Monmouth credits St Gildas and St Bede, as well as his friend Archdeacon Walter of Oxford. The latter, claims Geoffrey, provided a very ancient book (*Historia Brittonum*) as a source for the work. It is clear, however, that there is no historical basis for most of the contents; Geoffrey of Monmouth appears to have simply made up a good story and created a pseudo-history to support it.

Geoffrey of Monmouth starts his tale with Aeneas, a relative of King Priam of Troy. It is notable that many ancient legends suggest that the ancestors of Celtic people now native to the British Isles originated in Troy and either made their way directly to Britain or arrived by way of Greece, Italy or Spain. Geoffrey's Aeneas appears in Virgil's *Aeneid* as an ancestor of Romulus and Remus – the legendary founders of Rome. He apparently settled in Italy after various adventures in the Mediterranean along with his band of heroic companions.

Geoffrey of Monmouth's version of the several variants found in *Historia Brittonum* is that Britain came to be named after Brutus, the great-grandson of Aeneas. In some versions of this tale a seer predicted that Brutus would be a great man, and was put to death for saying so. Brutus was apparently banished after accidentally killing his father, and wandered through Europe before reaching an island named Albion. He is credited with founding the city of Tours along the way, but did not stay there.

Brutus reached Albion around 1100 BC, where he founded a city named Troia Nova. This became corrupted to Trinovantum and was later changed to London. In the meantime Brutus conquered Albion and divided it among his three sons upon his death. The names of these three sons are corrupted and applied to their three realms. Thus Logres (or Loegria) is England, Albany is Scotland and Kambria is Wales. These names appear in various places throughout the Arthur stories.

ABOVE: **The life of Aeneas after the fall of Troy is recorded in Virgil's *Aeneid*. According to legend, he was the ancestor of the founders of Rome and of Britain, and the ultimate cause of the Punic Wars between Rome and Carthage.**

This contains the first known reference to Arthur, but he is said to be a warrior rather than explicitly a king. Geoffrey of Monmouth redefines a number of characters from the *Historia Brittonum* as kings, so it may be that although Arthur does appear in the earlier work, Geoffrey of Monmouth is the first to mention 'King Arthur' and thus is the original creator of the myth.

The *Historia Brittonum* contains accounts of Arthur's battles against the Saxons, although no dates are given and some appear to be pure invention. There are also several versions of the stories contained within, which may reflect an attempt by more than one author to revise the tale in accordance with a personal agenda.

The *Historia Brittonum* claims to trace the origins of British kings all the way back to Trojan heroes, but also presents a bloodline for those heroes going all the way back to Noah. This is something of a contradiction, since Greek legend has the heroes descended from Greek gods while the *Historia Brittonum* traces their lineage to the Judeo-Christian Noah.

HISTORIA BRITTONUM GIVES THE KINGS OF BRITAIN A BLOODLINE GOING ALL THE WAY BACK TO NOAH.

At around the same time that Geoffrey of Monmouth was writing, a rival pseudo-history began to emerge which claimed that Scotland was founded by Scota, a Pharoah's daughter. This appears to be a counter to the *Historia Brittonum*'s claims that Scotland was essentially an offshoot of the Trojan-English kingdom. Be that as it may, *The History of the Kings of Britain* focuses mainly on the English kings, whose early deeds include a campaign in Gaul around 1000 BC. At that time Eburacus was King in Logres. He is credited with founding Eburacum (York) and constructing Edinburgh Castle. Most of his 20 sons went to Germany to found a new kingdom there.

Shakespeare's Inspiration

A notable descendent of Eburacus was Leir, whose father Bladud was a magician. Bladud is said to have practiced necromancy among other arts and tried to fly using artificial wings. After his death in the attempt, Leir became king. Leir is the basis for the Shakespeare play *King Lear*. The latter is a tragedy revolving around the aging King Lear splitting his kingdom rather unfairly between his daughters and gradually descending into madness. Some other versions of the play (both earlier and later variants of the same tale) have rather happier endings that match the version told in Geoffrey of Monmouth's *Historia Regum Britanniae*.

Among the descendants of Leir was Cunedagius, a contemporary of Romulus and Remus. This version of events would make London, York and Edinburgh Castle older than Rome. Cunedagius reunified Britain after a series of wars, and was followed by a series of kings about whom Geoffrey of Monmouth has little to say.

The next king of great significance was Gorboduc, whose two sons Ferrex and Porrex fought a civil war over who would inherit their father's kingdom. Ferrex survived an initial attempt on his life by his brother Porrex, fleeing to Gaul where he enlisted the help of the Frankish king. However, his invasion of Britain failed and he was killed in battle. The kingdom then collapsed into anarchy, with conflict between the classes of society as well as between the supporters of various factions. A play about these events, written in 1561, was a profound influence on the later work of Shakespeare and other Elizabethan playwrights.

This period of civil war is known as the War of the Five Kings, although exactly who these kings were remains uncertain, as do many events of the conflict. It came to an end when Dyfnwal

BELOW: The legendary King Leir fell victim to the false flattery of two of his daughters. The third, Cordelia, remained true to Leir and saved him when her sisters turned on their father. Shakespeare gave this tale an altogether more tragic ending.

Moelmud, King of Cornwall, defeated the King of Loegria and then formed an alliance of Cambria and Albany to reunify Britain. This lasted only until his death; his sons Belinus and Brennius then fought another civil war over the kingdom. The resulting peace settlement involved a kingdom split along the line of the River Humber on the east coast of northern England, with Belinus ruling the south and Brennius controlling everything to the north.

The compromise did not hold, and Belinus invaded the north. Brennius was aided by the King of Norway, whose daughter he had married, but the fleet he sent was attacked by ships from Denmark resulting in a sea battle. All of this is extremely unlikely, of course, not least because the kingdoms of Denmark and Norway did not exist at the time. A battle between fleets in the North Sea – in 400 BC – is also more than a little improbable.

Be that as it may, Geoffrey of Monmouth records that conflict continued until Brennius was finally defeated, leaving Belinus as King of the Britons. Brennius fled to Gaul and won the favour of the Allobroges tribe, finally becoming their ruler. He returned to Britain with an army of Gauls and continued the civil war for a time before a new peace settlement returned the brothers to their former territories. They then joined forces to invade and conquer Gaul, and forced a treaty on Rome. When the Romans broke this treaty, the brothers stormed Rome itself. Belinus returned to Britain while Brennius remained in Rome.

Gallic Sack of Rome

It is known that Rome was sacked – but not entirely conquered – by Gauls around 390 BC. The Gauls, according to traditional versions of the story, were led by one Brennus, chieftain of the Senones. It is extremely improbable that this individual was a British king, although there are other questions about the status of Brennus. It may be that he never existed at all, and instead was a legendary figure based on one or more real chieftains. If so then Geoffrey of Monmouth seems to have co-opted a Gaulish mythic figure and added him to the British legends.

ABOVE: Brennus, who led the sack of Rome, was probably a mythical figure who was later conflated with the equally mythical Brennius of Britain. Rome was, indeed, plundered by Gauls around 390 BC, but the identity of the Gaulish leader is open to question.

A series of kings followed Brennius and Belinus, and the deeds of these rulers at times tie in with other legends. For example, Gurguit Barbtruc is said to have encountered a large band of people fleeing from Spain after being exiled, and directed them to settle in Ireland. This parallels some Celtic myths that have Ireland settled by people crossing from Spain, although it contradicts others.

Around 340 BC, Britain was suddenly (and unaccountably) beset by monsters. King Morvidus, portrayed as a sort of benevolent psychopath, is recorded as defeating a giant, but later being slain by a dragon. There is perhaps a vague parallel to the old English tale of Beowulf in this account. Infighting and disputes among Morvidus' sons led to Britain being once again divided.

Many generations – about which Geoffrey of Monmouth has little to say – later, a king he refers to as Heli held the throne of Britain for about 40 years. Heli appears in Welsh mythology as Beli Mawr, an extremely important figure who was the

ABOVE: Cassivellaunus, who led the resistance to the initial Roman invasion of Britain, seems to have really existed – he is noted in Caesar's *Gallic Wars* – but his deeds in Geoffrey of Monmouth's version are mostly invented.

RIGHT: This dramatic representation of the Roman invasion features Celtic warriors driving their chariots into the sea, which seems more than a little unlikely as it would rob the Britons of the mobility that was their primary advantage.

grandfather of Lleu Llaw Gyffes. The latter is a great Welsh hero whose Irish equivalent is the equally impressive Lugh.

Heli's son was Llud Llaw Eraint, or Lud, after whom Trinovantum was renamed as Caer Lud. This was the origin of the modern name 'London' according to Geoffrey of Monmouth. Lud was succeeded upon his death by his brother Cassivellaunus, who led the Britons in their resistance to the Roman invasion of 54 BC. Cassivellaunus (spelled Cassibelaunus in the *Historia Regum Britanniae* and referred to as Caswallawn in Welsh literature, where he performs a number of additional heroic deeds) is mentioned in Julius Caesar's account, *Gallic Wars*, and is thus a historical figure. Geoffrey of Monmouth's account of his battles against Roman invaders is largely fictional, however.

The existence of at least some of the kings subsequent to Cassivelaunus is corroborated by historical evidence, although Geoffrey of Monmouth takes a creative approach to recounting their lives and deeds. Cunobelin, for example, is recorded as having good relations with Rome – an account that appears to be true. He is the basis of the Shakespeare play *Cymbeline*.

The conquest of Britain by the Roman Empire resulted in several of Geoffrey of Monmouth's kings becoming important figures in Roman history. In 202 AD, Septimius Severus, Emperor of Rome, campaigned against the Caledonian tribes in the hope of pacifying them. He failed, dying of illness at Eburacum (York)

in 211 AD to be succeeded as emperor by his sons Caracalla and Geta. The latter was soon murdered by his brother, who then ruled as sole emperor. In Geoffrey of Monmouth's version of events, Caracalla is referred to as Bassianus, and the feud between him and Geta results largely from the Roman desire to have Geta as emperor while the Britons preferred Bassianus.

The next Roman 'King of the Britons' was Carausius, who Geoffrey of Monmouth redefines as a Briton when in fact he was a Gaul. Geoffrey's account has Carausius given a Roman fleet to fight raiders from the coast of Germania, which instead he uses to oppose Bassianus and eventually kill him. Further Roman 'Kings of the Britons' follow, including the emperor Constantine the Great who was proclaimed at Eburacum in 306 AD.

Later Romano-British kings were involved in the power struggles of the late Roman Empire, in some cases challenging the existing emperor and in others simply seizing control of Britain. At the time of the Roman withdrawal from the British Isles, Geoffrey of Monmouth claims that Constans II was elected as King of the Britons. He was up to that point a monk, and made a rather poor king. This suited the purposes of Vortigern, one of the foremost chieftains among the Britons.

According to Geoffrey of Monmouth, Vortigern was the power behind Constans' throne until he eventually decided to dispose of him entirely. After instigating a treacherous murder, Vortigern ruled the Britons, but was dissolute and concerned mainly for the pleasures of the flesh. He rather unwisely invited the Saxons to fight as foederati against the Picts and Scots, resulting in large-scale Saxon pillaging when the arrangement broke down. Vortigern's negotiations with the Saxons resulted in them gaining

ABOVE: **Vortigern seems to have been a thorough villain who deposed the weak king Constans and then made a very bad deal with the Saxons. He received the blame for much of the misfortune that fell upon the Britons thereafter.**

additional land and thus power. He was deposed by his son Vortimer, who campaigned against the Saxons with some success. Vortimer is recorded as fighting several battles against the Saxons and greatly reducing their power, although others are at times credited with leadership in these engagements.

Treachery of the Long Knives

Vortimer's successes were undone after his death. Some accounts say he was murdered, but in any case Vortigern resumed his place on the throne and the Saxons returned. It has been claimed that Vortigern invited them, perhaps still hoping to use them as mercenaries, or it may be that he was simply powerless to stop their incursions. Vortigern's dealings with the Saxons led to an event known as the Treachery of the Long Knives, when Saxon leaders secretly brought weapons to a peace banquet and murdered their unarmed Briton counterparts.

Vortigern himself was captured and forced to cede large territories to the Saxons in return for his release. Having lost all of his strong places, Vortigern attempted to build a new fortress. This went awry, resulting in his meeting with the young Merlin, as related later. Thus Vortigern remained for a time a king, ruling a diminished realm from his new fortress in Cambria (Wales).

Vortigern was succeeded by Ambrosius Aurelianus, a Romano-British leader who is depicted differently in various accounts. According to Geoffrey of Monmouth, he was one of

VORTIGERN WAS CAPTURED AND FORCED TO YIELD LARGE TERRITORIES TO THE SAXONS.

the sons of Emperor Constantine III and brother to Constans. In some sources, Ambrosius' family were killed by Saxons; in Geoffrey of Monmouth's version, they were murdered by agents of Vortigern.

LEFT: According to legend, Stonehenge was constructed as a monument to the Briton leaders murdered by their Saxon counterparts in the Treachery of the Long Knives. Uther Pendragon was instrumental in obtaining the necessary stones from Ireland.

Wearying of both Vortigern and the Saxons, the remaining Britons selected Ambrosius to be their king and, with his younger brother Uther, he led them first against Vortigern. The latter burned to death in a tower where he took his last refuge from the besieging forces of Uther and Ambrosius.

AMBROSIUS AURELIANUS IS PROBABLY THE SAME PERSON AS RIOTHAMUS, WHOSE NAME MEANS 'GREAT KING'.

The Saxon leader Hengist was rightly frightened by Ambrosius' reputation as a warrior. He gave orders to fortify the towns of the Saxons, and made preparations to flee to Scotland if he was seriously threatened. Hearing that Ambrosius' army was approaching, Hengist attempted an ambush as Ambrosius marched to meet him, bringing about a large-scale battle that is depicted as a clash between the Christian Britons and the pagan Saxons.

Hengist was captured and later executed. His army had been defeated, but enough of the Saxons escaped to begin building a new force at York under Octa, son of Hengist and at Alclud under Eosa. These forces surrendered to Ambrosius after a time and were granted lands in the north of England. In the meantime, Ambrosius set about repairing damage to the churches and cities, restoring law to the country and returning the country to its ancient (and presumably rightful) state. According to Geoffrey of Monmouth, he was poisoned some time after his victory over the Saxons. His brother Uther became king after him, but in the meantime had a number of adventures.

Ambrosius wanted to raise a monument to the many Briton leaders slain in the Treachery of the Long Knives, and was advised by Merlin on what form it should take. This would be the stone circle known in modern times as Stonehenge. Stonehenge, of course, enormously predates these events, but Geoffrey of Monmouth probably did not know that – and he was not overly concerned with historical reality in any case.

The stones required to build the monument formed the Giant's Dance on Mount Killaraus in Ireland. Obtaining the correct stones required a campaign against the Irish under their young and valiant King Gillomanius. After defeating the Irish,

OPPOSITE: Uther Pendragon was a great war leader, but not a particularly good man. His lust for another man's wife led to war and magically-assisted adultery, which took place at the same time as Uther's former friend Gorlois was being killed in battle.

attempts were made to carry off the stones, but none could be moved until Merlin demonstrated how such huge weights could be handled using the right combination of devices.

Gillomanius sought revenge for his defeat, and agreed to attack the Britons in conjunction with some of Vortigern's remaining supporters. Uther led the campaign against them, since Ambrosius was at the time ill. While Uther was on campaign, Ambrosius was poisoned by a Saxon who pretended to be a monk and offered his services as a healer.

Uther Pendragon

Upon Ambrosius' death, a comet shaped like a dragon appeared and Merlin informed Uther of its significance. Henceforth Uther was named Pendragon. This name was probably derived from 'chief dragon', a traditional Welsh term for a great leader. He was a great warrior, a well-respected leader and a loyal supporter of his brother Ambrosius. He was not, however, without his flaws. His reign was characterized by conflict and violence, necessitating campaigns against Saxons and Scots as well as Irish invaders.

The violence began with an uprising among the Saxons in northern England. Octa (also referred to in some sources as Osla Big-Knife) and his kinsman Eosa had made a treaty with Ambrosius, but did not consider that it bound them after his

ABOVE: **Castle Pendragon in Cumbria is said to have been built by Uther Pendragon and to have served as his seat of government. The castle dates from the twelfth century, however; long after wars against the Saxons were over.**

death. The Saxons quickly overran large territories, and initially defeated Uther's army when he marched to oppose them. Taking refuge on Mount Damen, Uther launched a surprise counterattack and defeated the Saxons.

After this victory, Uther is recorded as pacifying Scotland and restoring law and order to the country, much as his predecessor had done. According to legend he built Castle Pendragon in Westmorland and made it his capital for much of his reign. Archaeology and modern historical research dates Castle Pendragon to the twelfth century, long after Uther's time. However, there are numerous local legends about Uther and his court surrounding the castle.

Uther's greatest ally up to this point was Gorlois (sometimes called Hoel), Duke of Cornwall. Gorlois had his seat at Tintagel and is variously referred to as Duke of Tintagel or of Cornwall. He was married to Igraine (sometimes called Ygerna), an extremely beautiful woman who was the mother of Gorlois' daughters. Sources vary on how many there were, some citing up to five, although not all are identified by name. Morgause married King Lot, Elaine (or Blasine) married Nuetres of Garlot, and Brimesent married King Urien. Another daughter, who is not named, appears in certain versions, and there is a fifth (who may be Morgana le Fay) in some accounts.

Gorlois was the architect of the great victory over the Saxons at Mount Damen, and the two returned in triumph at the head of their armies to Caer Lundein (London). At the celebration that followed, Uther met Gorlois' wife Igraine and became infatuated with her. Concerned at Uther's attitude (and perhaps advances) to his wife, Gorlois left the banquet. This was a breach of etiquette and an insult to Uther, who demanded that his former friend return and account for his actions. When Gorlois declined, Uther declared that he would destroy Gorlois if he did not surrender. Gorlois retired to his native Cornwall and began making defensive preparations.

At that time, Cornwall had two principal castles – his seat at Tintagel and another major castle at St Dimilioc. Gorlois placed Igraine in Tintagel Castle and readied himself for war at his other stronghold. After a period of conflict, Gorlois was defeated. However, Uther had become impatient and asked his friend Merlin for assistance in getting to Igraine. According to later versions of the tale, Merlin's condition was that any child born of the union would be placed in his care, which Uther accepted, but this is not mentioned in Geoffrey of Monmouth's version.

Uther's Magical Deception

Merlin used his magic to change Uther's appearance, making him appear to be Gorlois, and, with breathtaking cheek, Uther proceeded to Tintagel Castle where he was naturally given entry. In some versions of these events Gorlois was already dead; in others he was alive at the time that Uther visited Igraine, but was killed that same night.

Suspecting nothing, Igraine slept with Uther and conceived a son who would be named Arthur.

BELOW: Uther Pendragon is depicted here conspiring with Merlin to get into Tintagel Castle and see Igraine. Presumably Merlin considered that facilitating the conception of Arthur in this manner was worth a war with many deaths on each side.

This story raises questions about the legitimacy of Arthur's birth, although many versions claim that Gorlois was already dead at the time and that Uther's subsequent marriage to Igraine legitimized the child. Be that as it may, Arthur son of Uther was born as a result of a sorcerous deception, conceived by a man who was not Igraine's husband at the time – indeed, he was his enemy.

Arthur's conception at Tintagel is a central theme in the legends surrounding his life. Some versions focus on the magical nature of the deception, giving Arthur a semi-mystical side. Others seem to play on the fact that he was born of deception and treachery, leading perhaps inevitably to a tragic and doomed life.

When news came to Tintagel that Gorlois was dead, Uther was still there wearing his guise, and naturally quashed the rumours. He then left Tintagel and returned to the safety of his own army, later receiving the surrender of the castle. Soon afterwards Uther married Igraine, and Arthur was born at Tintagel.

The young Arthur was raised by Sir Antor, whose son Kay was Arthur's foster-brother and trusted companion. In the meantime Uther Pendragon continued to war against his many foes. His allies in this struggle included King Lot Lewddoc of Goddodin. King Lot eventually gave his name to Lothian, and may have had his seat at Edinburgh.

Lot was married to Morgause, who is referred to as Anna in some sources. Morgause is variously described as a daughter of Igraine and Uther (making her sister to Arthur) or of Igraine and Gorlois (making her his half-sister). According to some accounts Lot was for a time a hostage at Uther's court and met Morgause there, resulting in the illegitimate birth of Gawain. Lot was later an ally of Uther and campaigned on his behalf against the Saxons.

BELOW: **The baby Arthur was given to Sir Antor to raise alongside his own son Kay. Arthur was kept ignorant of his heritage, more than likely for his own safety. Being the heir to a kingdom would be a hazardous business.**

Uther Pendragon, by this time an old and sick man, was eventually drawn into a renewed campaign against the Angles of the north of England. Although defeated, they had been permitted to settle further north and were still ruled by Octa. Assisted by Saxons coming from Germany under their king, Colgrim, the Angles defeated Lot, who was commanding in Uther's name.

Uther took command of his forces and defeated Octa at St Albans and routed his enemies, although Colgrim managed to retreat to Eburacum. Uther died along with many of his foremost supporters as a result of a poisoned water supply and was buried at Stonehenge. Some sources claim the poisoning happened at Castle Pendragon, others during the late stages of his campaign against the Saxons.

LIKE OTHER KINGS OF ENGLAND BEFORE HIM, UTHER PENDRAGON DIED OF POISONING.

The Origins of Merlin

Merlin is a complex character who may have been based on a druidic magician. He is depicted in various different ways during the Arthurian legends, appearing at times as a very young or very old man, as something of a fool or as a wise counsellor, and even as a madman. It is possible that these tales originally referred to two entirely different men known by the same name, who were later conflated.

According to Geoffrey of Monmouth, Merlin was the grandson of a Welsh king, fathered by the Devil or an incubus (a demon). This is stated in the *History of the Kings of Britain* (1136), but in 1150 Geoffrey of Monmouth wrote *Vita Merlin* ('Life of Merlin') about an individual named Merlin Calidonius who was apparently married. There are no other mentions of Merlin being married.

The fact that Merlin's parents were servants of God and the Devil (or the Devil himself) granted him great power, as well as creating many contradictions. His royal blood may also have been a factor. He first appears as a boy, and his earliest interaction with a king is not Arthur or Uther, but Vortigern. The latter had fled to Wales after being heavily defeated by the Saxons, and was

LIFE OF MERLIN

The 1150 *Life of Merlin* contains a completely different version of events. In this tale, Merlin went mad with grief after a battle (possibly the Battle of Arfderydd) and lived as a wild man in the forest where he learned the speech of animals. He returned to sanity upon hearing music played by his sister Ganieda, who was married to Rodarch, one of the kings involved in the battle.

Merlin went to Rodarch's court, but was driven mad again by the presence of so many people. He ran wild in the woods, but was recaptured and brought back to court, where his sister looked after him. This care was rather poorly rewarded when Merlin told the court that Ganieda was having an affair. She dismissed this as the ravings of a madman, but Rodarch wanted proof of whether Merlin was mad or some kind of seer.

Merlin predicted that a boy at the court would die in a fall, because of a tree, and in water, which did not make much sense. He was permitted to return to the forest, which he did after telling his own wife that she should remarry. He added that he would visit on her wedding day and that her new husband should stay out of his way.

Soon afterwards, a boy died in the manner Merlin had predicted – falling from a rock he caught his feet in the branches of a tree and died of drowning as he dangled head-first in the river. King Rodarch realized that Merlin's warning about his wife's affair must be true and that he was indeed gifted with some kind of magical sight.

In the meantime, Merlin's ex-wife Gwendoloena planned to marry again. This went awry when she saw Merlin riding a stag amid a herd of deer that he was bringing to the court. She laughed, and her new husband went to see what was funny. For reasons that remain unclear Merlin broke off one of the stag's horns and threw it, killing Gwendoloena's new husband.

Merlin was brought back to court, where he demonstrated his ability to see things others could not. He also made some depressing predictions about future events. Among them was the prophecy that the mortally wounded Arthur would be taken to the Isle of Avalon, where he would be healed, but only if he remained there. Without him Britain faced an uncertain future, although Merlin predicted that Arthur would some day return to Britain. Eventually Merlin's sanity was restored by a magical spring. His role as lunatic-seer was taken over almost immediately by his sister Ganieda.

RIGHT: The *Life of Merlin* depicts Merlin as a gifted lunatic who spent much of his time running wild in the forest.

unsuccessfully trying to build himself a fortress. He was told by his advisers that he should find a boy without a father and use his blood to bind the mortar of his castle, as this would stop it from collapsing every night.

Merlin was duly found and brought to Vortigern, where he revealed that the real reason the castle kept collapsing was that two dragons were trapped under a pool of underground water that lay beneath the castle foundations. One dragon was red and one white, and their fighting caused the castle walls to crumble each night. The dragons then emerged from the ground and Vortigern witnessed them fighting one another. Merlin told him this was symbolic of the clash between Saxons and Britons.

Merlin revealed at this time that his name was Merlin Ambrosius (Emrys in Welsh), and Vortigern named the castle – which could now be completed – Dinas Emrys. Merlin's advice did not help Vortigern all that much, and after his death Merlin became friends with Ambrosius and Uther. The latter helped Merlin build Stonehenge, and it was Merlin who gave Uther the name Pendragon after they witnessed a dragon-shaped comet. Merlin facilitated Uther's seduction of Igraine and therefore the birth of Arthur, but in Geoffrey of Monmouth's account he plays no part in Arthur's reign.

In later versions of the Arthurian legends, Merlin appears as a mentor and adviser to Arthur, but he is absent in Geoffrey of Monmouth's telling of the tale. Various reasons for this exist, depending on the version of the tale being told. One variant has it that Merlin was trapped, imprisoned or entombed by a powerful sorceress referred to as the Lady of the Lake. Several quite different people are given this title in the Arthurian tales; this particular lady was a sorceress named Nimue, Niniane or Viviane with whom Merlin had become infatuated.

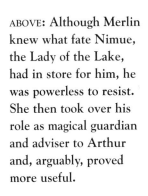

ABOVE: Although Merlin knew what fate Nimue, the Lady of the Lake, had in store for him, he was powerless to resist. She then took over his role as magical guardian and adviser to Arthur and, arguably, proved more useful.

The two first met when the lady was little more than a child. She wanted to learn the secrets of magic and promised Merlin her love if he would teach her. When they met again some years later, the sorceress imprisoned Merlin in an enchanted tower or entombed him in rock. In some versions of this tale the lady was suspicious of Merlin since she knew he was a child of the Devil, and was hostile to him. However, he was so infatuated that even though he foresaw his own demise at her hand he could not resist.

Although Niniane was inimical to Merlin, she helped Arthur on many occasions, notably after his sword Excalibur was stolen by Morgana le Fay. She was also one of the women who conveyed the mortally wounded Arthur to Avalon.

The Young Arthur

At the time of his father's death, Arthur was 15 years old, although this young age meant less in the past than it might today. In any case, there was little opposition to his assuming the throne of Uther Pendragon. The nobility of England were gravely concerned about the resurgence of Saxon power; meeting at Silchester, they agreed that Arthur should be king.

ARTHUR HAD THE SUPPORT OF THE BRITONS BUT THEY WERE BADLY OUTNUMBERED.

At that time, Saxons under the Germanic King Colgrim were rapidly overrunning Logres, and were soon in control of all the land north of the Humber. Fighting alongside Saxons native to Britain were new arrivals from the continent and also men from Ireland and Scotland who had voluntarily joined the Saxon cause or been compelled to do so.

Arthur was notable for being courageous and generous, qualities well liked by the nobility, and was generally thought of as a good and even-tempered man. Clearly, he had the makings of a popular and effective king, but his reign might be short-lived. Although he had the support of the Britons, Arthur was badly outnumbered.

Finances were also a possible problem. Arthur had wealth, and as Uther's son his right to rule was apparent. However, war was an expensive undertaking, as was maintaining the reputation for munificence that he was already creating. The answer to all

Arthur's problems was, of course, to make war upon the Saxons. Thus he would defend his people, cement the support of his lords and enrich them at the expense of their enemies.

Arthur marched first towards York and was met in the field by a large Saxon force under Colgrim, which was augmented by Irish, Scots and Picts. After a bloody battle, Colgrim was defeated and retired to York, where Arthur besieged him. Then, learning that 6000 more Saxons were approaching from the coast, Arthur sent a force to prevent them from breaking the siege.

Among his close supporters was Cador, named by Geoffrey of Monmouth as Arthur's cousin, but stated to be the son of Igraine

ABOVE: **This image of Arthur in battle shows the knights wearing great helms and using equipment from the thirteenth century. This is typical of the depiction of society in Arthur's time, though wildly anachronistic for a king fighting against Saxons.**

and Gorlois, which would make him a half-brother instead. Cador was the Duke of Cornwall (in the Welsh version of this tale he is Earl of Cornwall instead) and remained a staunch supporter of Arthur throughout his reign. Arthur sent Duke Cador to intercept the approaching Saxons, and despite being badly outnumbered, Cador staged a successful ambush on the road to York and routed the invaders.

However, Badulph, the leader of this new Saxon force, managed to trick his way into York in the guise of a jester, and soon afterward news arrived of a large force of Saxons landing on the coast. Unable to face such numbers, Arthur lifted the siege and retired towards London. There, he called a council at which it was decided to request aid from Hoel, Duke of Brittany. Hoel is variously cited as Arthur's nephew or his cousin, depending on the version of the tale, but in any case he was well disposed towards his kinsman and sent 15,000 men to his aid.

BELOW: Here, Arthur's links with the Church are emphasised. Later medieval writers were greatly concerned with the religious aspect of the story, placing piety and devotion to God as a virtue above duty to a knight's liege lord.

Arthur led his newly reinforced army into Lindsey (the marshy region lying between The Wash and the Humber Estuary, near modern-day Lincoln) where he overpowered a Saxon army and drove the survivors into nearby rivers. The remainder of the Saxon force rallied and made a fight of it at Celidon Wood, and so staunch was their defence that Arthur ordered a fortification to be made from chopped-down trees, fencing the Saxons in until hunger defeated them. This was a tactic used by Roman generals, and in this case it worked very well for Arthur.

Saxon Deception

The Saxons held out for a few days and then agreed to a peace settlement. They would return to Germany, leaving behind their treasures, and would in addition pay tribute to Arthur. Hostages were left behind as guarantee of good faith, and Arthur began to march north against the Picts and Scots. However, the Saxons broke their word as soon as they were at sea, returning to England and laying waste to the countryside. Arthur was forced to turn around and march south to deal with them; the hostages were executed as was the custom of the time.

The Saxons had reached Bath and were besieging it by the time Arthur caught up. Although his force was diminished, he resolved to break the siege and inflict a lasting defeat on the Saxons. Denouncing them as oathbreakers, and with the enthusiastic support of the clergy, Arthur led the attack. Among the inducements offered to Arthur's

ARTHUR BORE AN EXCELLENT SWORD NAMED CALIBURN.

men was the announcement of St Dubricius, who was with the army, that dying in this battle against treacherous heathens would absolve a man of any sins.

Geoffrey of Monmouth's account of the battle names Arthur's shield as Priwen, and states that he wore a golden helm in the shape of a dragon. His armour is described as being a coat of mail, which would have been fairly standard protection for a noble fighting man in 1136 when Geoffrey was writing – or around 500 AD, when these events supposedly took place. The plate armour often depicted in modern versions of the tale did not exist at either of these times. Arthur is also noted as bearing an excellent sword named Caliburn, which was made in Avalon, and a lance named Ron.

The Saxons, drawn up in a wedge formation, resisted the onslaught of Arthur's men for a whole day and retired to a hill to camp. The next day the diminished Saxons defended this hill, but were vigorously assaulted by Arthur's force. Geoffrey of Monmouth credits Arthur with slaying 470 Saxons (some other versions increase this to 960) single-handedly, and his troops also inflicted great slaughter. The Saxon brothers Colgrim and Badulph were killed, but Childeric, leader of the Saxon contingent from the continent, fled the battle.

After this great victory at Badon Hill, Arthur sent Cador, Duke of Cornwall, to pursue the remnant of the Saxon army with 10,000 men. Cador craftily got between them and their ships, and, having prevented their escape, began to harass and wear them down. Eventually, the remaining Saxons were cornered on the Isle of Thanet and compelled to surrender after Childeric was killed.

Arthur was in the meantime able to resume his march north, intending to rescue his kinsman Hoel who was besieged in Alclud. After rescuing Hoel, Arthur fought several battles against the Scots and Picts, causing them to flee to the islands of Loch Lomond. There, he denied them security by using the lake and surrounding rivers to move his forces by boat.

As Arthur conducted his siege of Loch Lomond, an Irish army under King Guillamurius approached. Arthur was obliged to lift his siege in order to defeat this new threat, but after driving off the Irish, he set about destroying the Scots and Picts once again. However, he was dissuaded by a delegation of holy men who asked for mercy in the name of their people.

The Scots and Picts wanted no further quarrel with Arthur, and said that they had been forced to fight against him by the Saxons, who had deposed their kings. Arthur granted a general pardon and, rather than further punishing the Scots, he reinstated their rulers. Among them was his father's friend King Lot, ruler of Lothian and husband of Arthur's sister (or half-sister) Morgause. Geoffrey of Monmouth states that Lot was King of Lothian, although some later sources refer to him as King of Orkney instead.

A DELEGATION OF HOLY MEN ASKED FOR MERCY IN THE NAME OF THEIR PEOPLE.

The King of Moray, north of Lothian, was Lot's brother Urien. Later legends instead make him King of Gorre, a mythical realm whose location can vary considerably. A third brother, Augusel, was King of Albany, the mythical name for Scotland. Geoffrey of Monmouth is rather vague about where the borders of Albany lay, but it seems clear that it was a major kingdom separate from Moray and Lothian.

At this time, Arthur's kinsman Hoel pondered the nature of Loch Lomond, and was informed by Arthur that it was indeed remarkable. He went on to say that other bodies of water existed that were equally or even more wondrous. Afterwards, the army went south and restored York, which had been ravaged by the Saxons. Geoffrey of Monmouth makes special note of the efforts to undo damage to holy buildings; his Arthur is a very pious man who shows great respect for the Church.

By accepting the fealty of the Scottish kings, Arthur further cemented his position as High King of Britain. However, significant resistance remained. Arthur planned a new campaign in the spring, but chose to spend the winter in Cornwall with Duke Cador. There, he met a young woman referred to by Geoffrey of Monmouth as Guanhumara, better known from other sources as Guinevere. The two were married soon afterwards.

Arthur Expands His Realm

At the time of his marriage to Guinevere, Arthur is described as having returned the land to its ancient state. This seems to suggest that he had brought under his control all the British lands formerly held by the Roman Empire. It may not be coincidental that Guinevere is described as being of Roman family; the

ABOVE: **Arthur's campaign around Loch Lomond prompted him to hold forth on the subject of magical bodies of water. It is not clear where he got this information – perhaps it was part of his tutelage from Merlin when he was a boy.**

ABOVE: **Arthur's marriage to Guinevere, who was from a noble family of Roman descent, may have been intended to symbolise his conquest of the formerly Roman territories in Britain.**

British King Arthur wed the best and most beautiful of Roman women just after making himself king of all the former Roman territories in Britain.

However, there was still a serious threat from the Irish under their King Guillamurius, so Arthur launched a major expedition to Ireland. Guillamurius met Arthur's force with a vast host, but his ill-disciplined and poorly armed followers were rapidly dispersed. Guillamurius was taken prisoner and surrendered to Arthur, after which the other rulers in Ireland soon surrendered.

Arthur, at least according to Geoffrey of Monmouth, then voyaged with his fleet to Iceland and subdued it. This is rather unlikely, since Iceland was probably not known to exist at the time. Norse sailors discovered Iceland in the ninth century, although there is some evidence that Irish monks had lived there for a time before that. Geoffrey of Monmouth's Arthur would have no difficulty subduing an uninhabited Iceland, but then neither would he have any reason to go there in the first place.

Arthur's reputation for invincibility and good rulership prompted some kings to voluntarily offer their allegiance. Gunfasius, King of Orkney, and Doldavius of Gothland came to offer tribute, joining many other kings in recognizing Arthur's overlordship. Thus began a 12-year period of peace in Britain, during which Arthur's court became famous and highly influential.

Arthur's court became a model for civilized society, attracting great and valorous people from all over Europe. Fashions among the nobility were influenced by what Arthur and his court wore, while warriors sought to imitate Arthur's knights (Geoffrey of Monmouth refers to them as such, even though it is something of an anachronism) in both equipment and deeds.

The End of Peace

Those kings who had not submitted to Arthur were awed and afraid of him, and made defensive preparations in case he chose to make war upon them. The 12-year peace ended when Arthur decided to do exactly that, beginning with the conquest of Norway. The Norwegian king, Sichelin, had named as his successor his nephew, Arthur's friend King Lot of Lothian. However, the Norwegians installed Riculf as their king instead.

Arthur sailed to Norway intending to overthrow Riculf and install Lot as king, and was met by a large Norwegian army when he landed. After a bloody battle Arthur killed Riculf and began a campaign to subdue all of Norway. When this was completed, Lot was installed as King of Norway, and Arthur sailed for Gaul.

Gaul was then under the control of a Roman tribune named Frollo, who assembled a huge army to oppose Arthur's landings. However, Arthur was accompanied by a large force of his own, made up of the best fighting men from all the lands he had gained. His men were young and keen to make a name for themselves, and Arthur's reputation also served him well. Many of those who came to fight against him asked instead to enter his service.

Frollo fled to Paris where he fortified himself and raised another army, but Arthur marched more quickly than expected and besieged the city. After weeks of starvation Frollo suggested to Arthur that in order to spare the people any more suffering they should fight a duel. This was gladly accepted, and with great pageantry the two met outside the city.

The encounter between Arthur and Frollo began on horseback, with Arthur unhorsing his opponent. As he closed in on the downed Frollo, the latter killed Arthur's horse with his lance. Arthur fell and was gravely threatened, but recovered himself to

BELOW: **After Frollo unsportingly killed Arthur's horse, the fight continued on foot. The matter was decided by powerful blows to the head – Arthur's helm withstood the impact; Frollo's did not.**

fight on foot. Despite taking a mighty blow to the helmet, Arthur clove through his opponent's helm and slew him.

According to the terms of the duel, the city of Paris then surrendered and Frollo's army was placed under Arthur's control. Half he gave to his kinsman Hoel, instructing him to pacify people referred to by Geoffrey of Monmouth as 'Pictavians'. This term is usually applied to the Picts of Scotland, but here it is a reference to the people of Aquitaine on the Bay of Biscay. The dominant Celtic tribe in the region before and during Roman times were the Pictones.

Hoel was opposed by Guitard, leader of the Pictavians, but defeated him after several battles and brought Aquitaine under Arthur's control. Hoel also campaigned in Gascony and forced its princes to submit. Arthur meanwhile subdued the rest of Gaul using the other half of Frollo's army, and nine years after landing in Gaul he held court at Paris. There, he placed trusted and loyal men in charge of the provinces of Gaul, before finally returning home to England.

RIGHT: A thirteenth-century depiction of Arthur's coronation as High King of Britain. Other kings retained their realms of course, but accepted Arthur as their liege. Given that he was at the height of his power, they really had no other option.

Arthur then held a great feast and celebration at the City of Legions. Geoffrey of Monmouth says that this was Caerleon in modern-day Monmouthshire, on the banks of the River Usk. Lords of great cities, kings and princes attended, along with high members of the clergy. Geoffrey of Monmouth lists a large number of dignitaries and adds that no prince worthy of consideration from anywhere in Europe outside Spain failed to attend.

AFTER THE BANQUET THE KNIGHTS HELD A TOURNAMENT THAT WENT ON FOR THREE DAYS.

At this celebration, Arthur was crowned. He had already received his father's crown, of course, but was now recognized as the High King over many other kings. After religious observances were complete there were two feasts – one for men and one for women. This was a tradition maintained since the days of ancient Troy, from whose heroes Arthur was descended.

Geoffrey of Monmouth expounds upon the splendour of the proceedings, stating that thousands of attendants – many of whom seem to be young noblemen – served the food at the banquet. He adds that fashion had become somewhat uniform, with knights dressing in similar manner and ladies also choosing their apparel based on the fashions of the court. Politeness and chivalry were now well established, and it was the custom that a lady would not give her love to a knight who had not fought well in at least three battles.

After the banquet the knights held a tournament, fighting on horseback while lesser men played sports and games. This went on for three days, with prizes offered for the victor in each of the many contests. On the fourth day, Arthur convened the nobles and clergy to bestow honours, rank and positions of authority upon his supporters.

War with Rome

While Arthur was bestowing honours upon his people, envoys from Rome arrived bearing a letter from Lucius Tiberius. Historically, at this time the Western Roman Empire had dissolved into a handful of rump states, although the Eastern

Empire still survived intact. Lucius is portrayed by Geoffrey of Monmouth as being a powerful ruler, however, and one that felt he had the right to command Arthur's submission.

Lucius' letter to Arthur accused him of failing to pay the tribute to Rome imposed by Julius Caesar hundreds of years previously, and of invading the lands of Gaulish tribes who were also tributaries of Rome. The latter accusation had some substance; Arthur had indeed conquered these lands. The withholding of tribute was scarcely a relevant issue any more. However, Arthur was commanded to present himself in Rome for judgement, and warned that war would ensue if he did not.

Arthur discussed the matter with Cador, who suggested that war with Rome might be a good thing. It would prevent the Britons becoming slothful and indolent, and provide an opportunity to win fame and glory. Addressing his nobles, Arthur asked for their opinions and stated that, while Lucius' demands were annoying, he was probably no real threat. The complaint that Arthur had invaded

ARTHUR PREFERRED TO REJECT THE ROMAN DEMANDS AND LET THE SWORD DECIDE.

the Roman area of interest in Gaul was not even worthy of an answer, Arthur stated, since Rome had abandoned those lands and made no attempt to defend them.

Arthur made it clear that he considered the demand for tribute to be unjust and perhaps rather silly, and that if Rome felt it had the right to demand tribute from Britain, then Britain could make a similar demand of Rome. He apparently considered that since he was a direct successor to the Roman governors of Britain then he was also a successor to the lords of Rome itself. This was not an unreasonable point of view; several very important figures in Roman history – including emperors – came from Britain.

Arthur's clearly stated opinion was that it was best to reject the demands and let the sword decide. However, he listened to the advice of his lords and made it clear that he preferred a unanimous decision on what to do. His lords, starting with Hoel, supported the idea. Hoel spoke of a prophecy that three Britons would rule the Roman Empire. Two – Constantine and Belinus – already had; Arthur would be the third.

LEFT: According to Geoffrey of Monmouth's tale, Arthur's campaign against Rome pitted his huge army against an enormous Roman force led by a large number of entirely fictitious kings.

Arthur's lords wholeheartedly agreed to the campaign against Rome and promised huge numbers of men. After giving instructions on where and when to assemble the host, Arthur met with the Roman envoys and told them that he was indeed intending to travel to Rome, but not to face any judgement other than that of battle.

The Romans, meanwhile, were gathering their own forces. Geoffrey of Monmouth's list of kings – many from the Middle East and North Africa – who sent forces to assist Rome is impressive and, of course, completely fictitious. The Roman

Empire of a few centuries previously might have assembled such a force, but the remnant in Italy could not even defend itself properly against barbarian incursions.

Arthur left his kingdom under the governance of Queen Guinevere and Arthur's nephew Modred (Mordred), who was the son of King Lot. During the final preparations for the campaign Arthur dreamed of a battle between a dragon and a flying bear. Various interpretations were offered, but, since Merlin played no part in Arthur's life in this version of the tale, there was no definitive advice available.

While the army waited for all its contingents to arrive, news came that a giant from Spain had taken prisoner Helena, niece of Duke Hoel and was now ensconced atop St Michael's Mount. The giant seemed unassailable; he could capsize ships and hurled rocks or darts at soldiers who approached.

ARTHUR LEFT HIS KINGDOM UNDER THE GOVERNANCE OF GUINEVERE AND HIS NEPHEW MORDRED.

Arthur resolved to deal with the giant and set off with only his closest companions. Arriving too late to save Helena, Arthur was still able to surprise the giant in his camp, and endeavoured to prevent him from picking up his huge club. In this he was unsuccessful and was dealt a mighty blow. In return, Arthur stabbed the giant in the forehead, blinding him with his own blood so that he ran onto Arthur's sword. The severed head of the giant was taken back to the army and displayed to Arthur's men.

Having assembled his forces, Arthur advanced and camped close to the army of Lucius Tiberius, sending envoys to order the Romans to withdraw or face the Britons and their allies in battle. The meeting did not go well, with the Romans insulting the Britons and a fight subsequently breaking out. The diplomatic party was forced to make a fighting retreat.

The pursuing Romans were then assailed by 6000 Britons and put to flight, which was reversed when 10,000 Romans joined their countrymen. More reinforcements arrived to assist the Britons, and a large-scale battle ensued in which the superior discipline and better tactics of the Romans began to tell. Seeing this, the Briton commanders charged through the

Roman army and began fighting with its commander. The fight then degenerated into a general free-for-all in which the Roman commander was captured.

The disorganized Romans were finally broken by a charge of the Britons, whose commanders then reported to Arthur that they had begun a battle without permission, but managed to win it. Arthur was pleased with their performance and ordered the Roman prisoners taken away under guard. As they marched away from the battle area, the escort was attacked by 15,000 Romans. Despite a gallant defence, the Britons faced defeat until the king of the Pictavians came up with part of his force, having heard of the Romans' stratagem, and inflicted a defeat on the ambushers.

These defeats demoralized Lucius Tiberius, who began a retirement towards Augustodunum. Arthur marched to intercept him, dividing his force into seven components of equal size, as well as a reserve in case the day went badly. He gave orders to engage the enemy directly with infantry, while the cavalry

LEFT: **Arthur is recorded as personally decapitating two of the kings on the Roman side, but unusually for such a tale he did not engage the Roman commander, who was slain by an unknown opponent.**

attempted a flanking movement to disorder the enemy. These preparations made, Arthur made a final speech to his army.

Hearing of Arthur's preparations, Lucius Tiberius decided to halt his retreat and marched to engage the Britons. He, too, made a rousing speech. The armies drew up in order of battle, with the Romans launching the first charge. Other divisions of each force were drawn in until a huge battle raged in which many great deeds were done and notable men fell on both sides.

At the height of the battle, the Britons made a heroic attempt to kill Lucius Tiberius, who was for a time personally engaged in combat. The assault was eventually thrown back, and the tide began to turn against Arthur's force. At this juncture, Arthur drew his sword Caliburn and exhorted his men to valour, charging into the Roman force and decapitating two of their kings. Even though no one who came within reach of Arthur's sword survived, the issue remained in doubt until the Britons' final reserve attacked the Roman rear. Lucius Tiberius was killed by an unknown hand, and the Roman force finally broke.

The Britons pursued the remnants of the Roman army, killing those who did not surrender themselves, before sending the body of Lucius Tiberius to the Senate with a message that this was the only tribute Arthur would be sending. The Britons did not march into Italy, however. Instead Arthur busied himself with reducing the strongholds of the region. In the spring, as he prepared to march into Italy, Arthur received grave news from Britain.

Arthur and Mordred

In some variants of the Arthurian legends, Mordred is Arthur's illegitimate son, but in Geoffrey of Monmouth's version he is the child of King Lot and Arthur's sister (or half-sister) Morgause. Left to govern Briton, Mordred had seized Arthur's throne and married Guinevere. This seems to have been consensual on her part, making them both traitors.

Mordred set about securing his new kingdom by gathering an army made up of Arthur's enemies. Troops came from Ireland, Scotland and Pictland, but most notably from among the Saxons of Germania. These had been promised the lands in England that they had held in the time of Vortigern and Hengist.

When Arthur and part of his army landed in England they were immediately attacked and suffered great losses, before driving off the enemy. The decisive factor seems to have been Arthur's tactic of making a frontal engagement with his infantry then sending the cavalry in obliquely, disordering the opposing force. Mordred fell back to Winchester and began to reform his army while Guinevere fled to a nunnery.

Arthur besieged Mordred, who sallied out with his army to break the siege. He was defeated after a bloody battle and began a retirement towards Cornwall, while Arthur marched in pursuit. At the Cambula River, Mordred made a final stand, bringing about the clash normally referred to as the Battle of Camlann.

Arthur divided his force up as he had during the war against Rome, creating nine divisions. Mordred divided his army of 60,000 into four parts. Three contained 6666 men each, with the whole of the remainder in a single group under Mordred's personal command.

The forces were evenly matched, resulting in a day-long slaughter that ended only when Arthur led his personal force (also numbering 6666 men) directly at Mordred's position.

ABOVE: **The Battle of Camlann was an epic bloodbath, with kings, famous knights and other notables slain on both sides. Mordred was killed in the fighting, but this did not unduly discourage his followers. Arthur won the battle, but at the cost of a mortal wound.**

Arthur led his men in breaking through the enemy line, but even when Mordred was slain his force battled on. Geoffrey of Monmouth lists numerous kings, leaders and notables slain in the fighting, and Arthur himself was mortally wounded.

ABOVE: **In this version of the encounter between Arthur and Mordred, Arthur did not use Caliburn, but instead impaled Mordred with a spear. Mordred died on the field of battle; Arthur lived long enough to see victory.**

After Arthur's Death

Dying, Arthur named as his successor Constantine, son of Duke Cador of Cornwall. Geoffrey of Monmouth states rather matter-of-factly that Arthur was then carried to the Isle of Avalon to be cured of his wounds. Constantine, meanwhile, assumed the throne of the Britons in 542 AD, and immediately had to deal with an insurrection led by the two sons of Mordred. These fled when they were defeated, seeking sanctuary on holy ground. Constantine captured them and put them to death without trial. More importantly, these murders were carried out on holy ground.

Saxons were also an ongoing problem, and Constantine fought several battles with them during his short reign. He was killed by his nephew Aurelius Conan three years after killing the sons of Mordred; Geoffrey of Monmouth states that God's vengeance pursued him.

Constantine was buried alongside Uther Pendragon at Stonehenge, and Aurelius Conan took the throne. Geoffrey of Monmouth states that he was very courageous but delighted in civil war. His efforts gained him the throne, but only briefly; he died after two years.

Subsequent kings were greatly troubled by Saxons arriving in huge numbers from the continent. Although they were valiant and sometimes successful, the golden age of Arthur's reign did not return, and Britain became too weak to resist invasion. In the reign of King Careticus an alliance between the Saxons and the King of the Africans, who had invaded Ireland, laid waste to the entire country. Cities were razed, and so bad was the destruction that Geoffrey of Monmouth states that almost the whole surface of the island had been burned up.

The Britons were forced to retire to remote places and to seek what safety they could, while Logres became the dominion of the Saxons. The history of Britain – Geoffrey of Monmouth's version of it, anyway – continues beyond this point, but the time of King Arthur and the greatness of the Britons was truly over. After Arthur came a collapse into civil war, paganism and disaster that counterpointed the chivalrous golden age of his reign.

None of it happened, of course, except in the most general of terms, but Geoffrey of Monmouth wove a tale of better, heroic times that still appeals to the reader today. His legend tells of a bright time of glory still remembered on the far side of the darkness that came after. Others took the tale and added to it, but Geoffrey of Monmouth gave us the original.

BELOW: Arthur was taken to the Isle of Avalon to be healed of his wounds. Behind him he left a Britain much diminished by his passing. Soon, all Arthur's work would be undone and all that would remain was a bright legend.

3

THE ROMANCES

The tale of King Arthur, as told by Geoffrey of Monmouth, is a fairly straightforward one of battles against the Saxons and other foes. There is the occasional giant or dragon, but for the most part it is a political thriller rather than an action-hero adventure.

Geoffrey's Arthur is a dynamic, inspirational leader who fights for his kingdom and is ultimately betrayed through no fault of his own. There is little focus on individuals other than Arthur in this version of the tale. No mention is made of questing knights, there are few supernatural events during Arthur's life, and many of the elements today considered by many to be at the heart of the legend are not present. The quest for the Holy Grail, the sword in the stone and the apparently central idea of a Round Table of knights were all later additions.

The first new version of the Arthurian legend was published in 1155, not long after the original. Written by the poet Wace,

OPPOSITE: **The round table at Winchester Castle was made around 1250, and was redecorated in the reign of Henry VIII. This was probably done for a Round Table tournament, in which participants took on the role of various Arthurian characters.**

it was entitled *Roman de Brut*. This was a translation of Geoffrey of Montmouth's *Historia Regum Britanniae* into Norman verse for the new overlords of Britain. Wace retold Geoffrey's story all the way from the founding of Britain by Brutus, and he added the concept of the Round Table.

ABOVE: The poet Wace lived most of his life in Normandy, and lived long enough to see the Norman conquest of England. He wrote the *Roman de Brut* around 1150–1155, renaming Arthur's sword Excalibur, but otherwise generally following Geoffrey of Monmouth's version.

The idea of the Round Table was really quite radical in the Middle Ages, where precedence was extremely important. If a lord had many guests, the most senior were given the best accommodation. Those further down the social order were granted a place to sleep in the great hall, with the highest ranked getting the best spots close to the fire.

At dinner, the most senior guests sat at the high table with the host, with the most prominent among them being closest to him. If there was a single table, the host sat at its head with the highest ranked of his guests closest. Being sat 'higher' (i.e. closer to the host or the head of the table) was a sign of precedence and was the cause for much bickering among noblemen of generally equal rank.

Code of Conduct

The court of King Arthur, as described by Geoffrey of Monmouth and expanded upon by Wace, was a place of chivalry and honour. The best and noblest aspired to join the Knights of the Round Table, while notables from other kingdoms came there for political purposes. It was a fine setting for romances of heroism and chivalry, and could be home to many fascinating characters whose adventures took place against the backdrop of the original Arthurian legend.

The stage was now set for the great Arthurian romances; a new genre of writing pioneered by the French poet Chrétien de Troyes (1130–1191). It was he that introduced the Grail Quest and even Camelot itself; Lancelot is another creation of his. The needs of the story caused him to tweak a few details here and there – his Arthur is not quite so dynamic as that of Geoffrey of Monmouth, and is at times a rather weak monarch whose subjects can more or less do as they please. Thus crises that would more than likely have been dealt with personally (and with great vigour) by Geoffrey's Arthur require the attention of Chrétien's other heroes. In some of the new 'Arthurian' tales, Arthur is the key character; in others, his story provides a backdrop for the deeds of others.

A SYMBOL OF UNITY AND EQUALITY

Precedence was extremely important for social, political and military reasons, but it was also divisive among men who were supposed to be comrades and friends. By creating a Round Table at which none sat above another – not even Arthur – much of the tension arising from precedence disputes was allayed. It could be argued that some were still sitting closer to Arthur than others, but the symbolism was of unity and equality.

Given that kings, for very good and necessary reasons, placed themselves above others and were highly concerned about maintaining their station, Arthur's decision to be at the same level as his knights might seem strange. It was certainly not a concept that most Medieval kings would – or could – consider. A king who treated his high nobles as equals might find his authority over them eroded.

Of course, Arthur extended the privilege of membership of the Round Table to only the best and most loyal of knights. He was the first among equals in a fellowship of those who had proven their loyalty and worth, and held his position out of respect he had earned rather than forcing his authority upon his subjects – at least in theory. In practice some of the Round Table Knights did betray Arthur or acted against his best interests, making theirs a betrayal of friendship as well as treason against their king.

LEFT: **Many of the Knights of the Round Table were kings in their own right, but any knight of the table was the equal of any other.**

The first of Chrétien de Troyes' poems concerns the life of Sir Erec, a Knight of the Round Table. Holding court at Cardigan, King Arthur decided that he would like to hunt the white stag. This was more than a mere hunt, as the white stag was thought to have supernatural properties. This idea probably came from the ancient Celtic tradition that the beast was connected with the otherworld.

Arthur was warned that no good could come of this hunt, since tradition required whoever caught the stag to kiss the fairest lady of the court. This would inevitably cause a disagreement among the 500 ladies present, and more importantly their husbands and lovers. Arthur acknowledged this but decided to proceed anyway.

Erec, who was a very great and well respected knight, did not take part in the hunt but instead kept the queen and her maid company, while King Arthur and his men dashed in pursuit of the stag. When the hunt had moved far off, Guinevere spotted a strange knight approaching and sent her maid to ask who he might be. The maid tried to do so, but was chased off by the knight's servant, a dwarf, who struck her with a whip.

Sir Erec was then sent to speak to the knight, but was also struck by the dwarf's whip. He withdrew to the queen, unable to strike the dwarf without fighting his knightly master. Erec was at that time unarmed and unarmoured, and believed the strange knight would kill him given the slightest provocation. The knight rode off, and Erec went in pursuit, intending to somehow obtain arms on the way.

Meanwhile, Arthur had killed the stag and must now kiss the fairest lady of the court. This caused a disturbance among the knights and nobles of the court, and Arthur asked his nephew Sir Gawain for advice on how to quell it. A council was called, attended by the best and boldest, including kings and princes, to discuss how to resolve the matter, but when Guinevere told Arthur of the incident earlier it was decided to postpone the kiss until Sir Erec returned.

ARTHUR WAS WARNED THAT NO GOOD COULD COME OF THIS HUNT.

Following the strange and villainous knight, Sir Erec
came to a town where he sought lodging with a courteous but
impoverished *vavasor*. This term is rather vague in meaning and
usually refers to a nobleman somewhere below a knight in rank.
The vavasor's daughter was extremely beautiful, but content to
remain in poverty until a worthy suitor appeared.

The strange knight was one of many attending a fête at the
town, and the vavasor loaned Erec his arms in order to enter it.
Erec revealed his identity, saying that his father was King Lac and
that if the vavasor's daughter found him suitable, then one day
she would be the wife of a king. This was agreeable to everyone,
so the next day Erec was able to enter the fête. Among the events
was a contest to win a sparrowhawk, a prize that was awarded to
the knight that was accompanied by the fairest lady.

ABOVE: A depiction of
Arthur hunting from
around 1300. Hunting
was more than sport;
it promoted a martial
and adventurous spirit.
Hunting also involved
a great deal of physical
exercise and no little
risk.

Duelling Knights

The contest brought Erec into conflict with the strange knight, and after an exchange of hard words they charged at one another with lances. Unhorsed, they then battled with swords until both were exhausted. Unable to strike hard enough to injure each other, the two knights became embarrassed about how long their duel had gone on for and agreed to stop for a rest.

After resting for a while they set to once more, hacking each other's shields to pieces and penetrating armour to strike telling blows. Finally, Erec knocked his opponent down and was about to despatch him when the other knight begged for mercy. Erec explained why he fought with such hatred, and demanded of the strange knight that he go to the queen immediately to answer for the harm done to her maid.

The knight, whose name was Yder, did so and surrendered himself to the queen. He confessed to what had happened, and that he had been beaten by Sir Erec. Guinevere said that his punishment should be lighter as he had behaved honourably since his defeat, but Arthur ruled that if Yder would join his court he would not be punished at all.

Erec, meanwhile, celebrated his great victory with the people of the town and their lord, and made preparations to elevate the impoverished vavasor to high station in his father's kingdom. He then returned to court where he was greeted by the king, queen and many notables.

At this point in the tale, Chrétien de Troyes makes much of the rich clothing and gifts bestowed upon Erec's bride-to-be by the queen, and when she is presented to the court he names many of the Knights of the Round Table. First among these, he says, is Gawain, and Erec second. Lancelot is named third.

Arthur cleverly decided to bestow the delayed kiss upon Erec's betrothed, which caused no dissent.

Erec kept his word to the vavasor, and sent him many rich gifts. He also petitioned King Arthur to allow him to be married at court, which was granted. Finally, the name of Erec's betrothed was revealed – she was named Enide – and the two were married by the Archbishop of Canterbury.

The wedding was a huge affair, followed by weeks of celebration and a tournament. Chrétien de Troyes describes this in a way that suggests it

AN UNHORSED KNIGHT WOULD BE ATTACKED AS HE TRIED TO GET TO HIS FEET.

was not the formal joust for prizes of the later Medieval period but a violent business where an unhorsed knight would be attacked as he tried to get to his feet. Knights fought until forced to surrender, and then owed a ransom to their captor.

This sort of tourney was a dangerous business, and in it Erec showed his prowess. Demolishing two notable knights with his lance, he met with the King of the Red City. After both had smashed their lances, Erec defeated his opponent but did not stop to take his ransom, so keen was he to demonstrate his fighting skills on a new opponent.

By the end of the tournament, Erec had shown himself to be the best of all the competitors, but soon afterward he left to return to his home country where he was very well received. However, Erec and Enide were so content in their marriage that soon Sir Erec, who Arthur had considered surpassed all but Gawain of his Round Table companions, lost interest in martial pursuits.

Soon, rumours began that Erec was a coward. He remained ignorant of

BELOW: **The knights in this depiction of a tourney are equipped in late Medieval style, with plate armour that was likely reinforced specifically for the joust. Jousting in chain mail was far more hazardous, and occasionally fatal.**

this, but Enide knew what was being said. At first, she withheld it from him, but felt increasingly guilty that this greatest of knights was spoken of in this manner, and was no longer the hero he had once been. Eventually she let slip what she was thinking, causing Erec to take action.

Erec immediately put on his armour and rode out with his wife, refusing to take any companions with him. He instructed Enide not to speak to him unless spoken to first. As she rode ahead of her husband, she spotted three knights who clearly planned to ambush him. After a moment's indecision, Enide disregarded her husband's instructions and called out a warning to him.

Erec Under Attack

Chrétien de Troyes describes the ensuing fight in fairly graphic and exciting manner. This is very much an action-adventure story, not a history of legendary kings. Notably, the three knights – even though they make their living by robbery and ambush – adhere to the code of the time and attack one at a time. Ganging up was bad form even for robbers, it seems.

BELOW: **The popular image of an Arthurian tournament was largely shaped by books such as the 1910** *Gateway to Tennyson,* **which featured this illustration. Tennyson's work was loosely based on the original Arthurian romances.**

After the fight Erec warned Enide that she must never again defy him by speaking without being spoken to. She agreed, but when a band of five knights approached intent on robbery she once more called out a warning. Erec told her that she has earned no gratitude by her actions, and again warned her not to defy him.

Later in their journey, the count of a town where the two stayed the night offered to rescue Enide from her present predicament. Even though she was miserable – with good reason, for her husband was treating her rather badly – she declined the offer. This angered the count, who threatened to have Erec murdered in front of his wife. She offered a different plan, one that would make the incident appear less dishonourable, and promised herself to the count.

After agonizing about the decision to again speak to her husband, Enide told him of the count's treachery. The two slipped away, but were pursued by the count and 100 of his knights. Erec decided to fight all of them rather than flee, killing the count's seneschal and badly wounding the count himself. Repenting of his treachery, the count ordered his men to cease their pursuit.

After this, Enide again warned her lord of approaching danger, despite fearing his anger. This time it was a fearsome knight who wished to test himself against the passing stranger. Both were wounded in the first pass with lances, but continued their fight on foot with swords for the next six hours, while Enide looked on, distraught that she might lose her husband.

EREC DECIDED TO FIGHT ALL ONE HUNDRED OF THEM RATHER THAN FLEE.

Breaking his sword, the strange knight was forced to surrender and Erec demanded his name. He revealed that he was Guivret the Little, and was king of the surrounding country. He desired Erec to become his friend and offered hospitality, which Erec declined. Guivret did agree to send aid if Erec ever asked it of him, and after bandaging up one another's wounds, the two parted.

Next, Erec and Enide came upon the court of King Arthur. They were greeted by Sir Kay, Arthur's seneschal, who did not recognize Erec. A dispute arose, leading to a joust in which Sir Kay was bested, so Arthur sent Sir Gawain to invite this strange knight to be his guest. Erec refused, but while Gawain stalled him in conversation, Arthur had his entire camp moved so that it was directly in Erec's path. Outwitted, Erec revealed his identity and was warmly received by his former comrades.

Erec insisted on travelling onwards the next day, refusing to stay at Arthur's camp. Soon he encountered a lady whose lover had been taken captive by two giants. Moved by her distress, Erec resolved to rescue her knight and went in pursuit. Catching up, he scolded the giants for their cruel treatment of their captive. When they refused to release him, Erec issued a challenge.

After killing the giants, Erec sent the knight he had rescued, Cadoc of Tabriol, to seek out King Arthur and tell him what had happened. By the time he returned to Enide, Erec's wounds had

ABOVE: **The court of King Arthur followed him wherever he went. He might hold court at one of his own castles, the castle of a friend with whom he was staying, or in a temporary camp on the road somewhere.**

reopened and he collapsed, causing her to fear him dead. She considered killing herself to end her grief but was prevented by a party of knights who bore Erec to their town.

The lord of the town, Count Oringle of Limors, offered to make Enide his wife, and tried to get her to eat. She would not, and defied the count even when struck and threatened. At this juncture, Erec awakened from unconsciousness and came to his wife's rescue, routing the knights and killing their lord. As the two made their escape, Erec told Enide that he no longer had any doubts about her love and loyalty.

Guivret the Little, distressed at hearing rumour that his new friend had been killed, assembled 1000 men-at-arms to accompany him to Limors. There, he would storm the town and take Erec's body if the count would not surrender it, so highly did he think of Erec. His force encountered Erec and Enide at night, and failed to recognize them, so Guivret and Erec fought another duel.

This one was short, for Erec was already half-dead. When Erec collapsed from his injuries, Enide tried to protect him. She chastised Guivret for attacking an exhausted man, and he agreed to stop if she would tell him who they were. Guivret then apologized to his

friend for the misunderstanding and the fight, and was forgiven.
Erec and Enide stayed with Guivret until Erec was healed, and
discovered that their love for one another was greater than
ever. Further adventures are recounted in the remainder of
the tale, until at last Erec and Enide returned home to inherit
the kingdom of Erec's father. However, these come after the
resolution of the story's main driving theme – the tension
between Erec and Enide.

This tale is perhaps a model for many other Arthurian
adventures. Many elements are repeated elsewhere, including
enemies who become friends through the hard courtesies of
honourable combat, and strangely intractable heroes whose
actions sometimes make little sense. For example, Erec and
Guivret need only to have spoken a couple of words to avoid
their second fight, but for some reason remained silent instead.
Erec's treatment of Enide is also open to a certain amount of
questioning.

The story is clearly intended to entertain in the
manner of an action novel or movie. It is littered
with lurid descriptions of helms shorn through,
while swords and lances frequently penetrate mail
and the vital organs beneath. Honour and the
customs of knighthood are also prevalent – even
among giants and robbers. Knights play by the
rules, and when outmatched, Erec still follows the
code of honour rather than sneakily trying for an
unfair advantage.

Most of all, though, this is a tale of courtly love.
It is unusual in that the lovers are actually married
to one another; more commonly an ill-fated affair
takes place between a knight and someone else's
wife. However, the driving force in this tale is
romance, and the rather odd choices made in its
name. The story of Erec and Enide has a happy
ending – despite being tested to the limits, Enide shows her
loyalty to her lord, and he battles all comers to protect her, before
finally returning home with her as his queen. Other Arthurian
romances do not turn out quite so well for their protagonists.

BELOW: The ideal of
courtly love – if it
existed at all – helped
raise the status of
knights above that
of rough men of war.
Anyone could fight; it
was the manners and
courtesies of the knight
that made him special.

Cligès

Published in 1176, *Cligès* is the second of Chrétien de Troyes'
poems. It is in two main parts, the first of which concerns the
doings of Cligès' father and the second of Cligès himself. The
father was named Alexander, and he was the son of the Emperor
of Greece and Constantinople. His was a noble and honourable
line, but rather than become a knight in his home country, he
resolved to journey to the court of King Arthur.

Alexander was so impressed by what he had heard of Arthur's
court that he promised to wear no helmet until knighted by
Arthur himself. He was given a huge
amount of money to take with him to
England, but the emperor also extolled
the virtues of a noble man, of which
generosity was the foremost.

Arriving in Southampton in a
horribly seasick state after a long voyage,
Alexander and his companions sought out King Arthur and were
told he was at Winchester. Chrétien de Troyes makes much of the
noble qualities of the Greeks – they were young and handsome,
courteous and well behaved, and thus pleasing to the civilized
court of Arthur.

> ALEXANDER VOWED TO
> WEAR NO HELMET UNTIL
> KNIGHTED BY ARTHUR
> HIMSELF.

Alexander and his friends were made welcome at court,
and Alexander himself became great friends with Sir Gawain.
Naturally, he was included in a party accompanying Arthur to
Brittany, and while aboard ship he met a maiden in the service of
the queen, named Soredamors. Soredamors was the sister of Sir
Gawain and had no interest in love whatsoever.

Finding herself attracted to Alexander, Soredamors was
tormented by her feelings. Not knowing that Alexander felt the
same, she suffered this way for some time. Queen Guinevere,
seeing the two of them terribly afflicted by some malady, assumed
they were both very seasick until the party landed in Brittany.

Chrétien de Troyes goes on at length about the torments
caused by the love of Soredamors and Alexander for one another.
They remained in Brittany with Arthur's court for some months,
and suffered through every night and day. Finally, word came that
Count Angres of Windsor, chosen by Arthur to rule England in

his absence, had betrayed his king and raised an army against him.

Arthur raised what Chrétien de Troyes describes as the largest army the world has ever seen, and set sail for England. Alexander and his companions asked to be knighted so that they could join the battle, and Arthur agreed. While the king furnished arms and harness, Queen Guinevere also wished to give a gift to Alexander and gave him a silk shirt with golden stitching. Alexander did not know it, but Soredamors had stitched the shirt and used some of her own hair in place of the gold threads.

At the approach of Arthur's gigantic army, Count Angres fled to Windsor Castle – but not until he had thoroughly plundered London. Secure in their fortress, which had been strengthened all summer in anticipation of this situation, Count Angres' knights were unafraid of Arthur's forces and came out to practice jousting in full view of their enemies.

ABOVE: **A fifteenth century depiction of Arthur and his knights arriving at a castle. The occasional Royal Progress around the kingdom helped remind the nobility that they were not beyond the reach of the king.**

Seeking to make a name for himself, Alexander led his companions across a ford to attack the enemy knights, and, after an initial clash of lances, he put them to flight. After a brief rampage among the dismayed enemy, Alexander returned to camp with four captive knights. Arthur wanted to execute them immediately, so Alexander surrendered them to Guinevere instead.

While Arthur and Guinevere were arguing about the fate of the captives, Soredamors noticed that Alexander was wearing the shirt that she had made. As she was pondering the implications of this Alexander was informed that his actions had pleased the king and that he was to be assigned a body of troops to command. When the battle was over, Arthur promised him the best kingdom in Wales as his own fief.

The assault on Count Angres' stronghold made little headway, despite being conducted with great vigour. Chrétien de Troyes describes the use of slings and crossbows along with javelins and stones hurled from engines. Seeing that no progress was being made, Arthur offered a rich reward to whoever could bring the siege to a successful conclusion.

Meanwhile, Alexander was in the habit of visiting the queen, who noticed that the gold thread in his shirt was tarnishing, but the hairs put there by Soredamors were becoming even more shiny. She made Soredamors tell Alexander that she had made the shirt, which delighted him – but still the two could not speak of their love.

RIGHT: A fifteenth century depiction of Guinevere under siege. The attackers are equipped with a bombard: a primitive cannon of little use in the field but excellent for destroying castle walls.

Early the next morning, Count Angres and his men made a desperate push to attack the camp of Arthur while his knights were still sleeping. They were detected in time for Arthur's men to arm themselves, and a luridly described battle took place in which Alexander greatly distinguished himself. At last, Count Angres fled back towards his fortress with a handful of his knights. Alexander instructed his men to take equipment from dead enemies, making his force look like they, too, were fleeing the battle.

ALEXANDER AND HIS MEN BLUFFED THEIR WAY INTO THE FORTRESS AND FELL UPON THE COUNT WITHOUT WARNING.

Feigning weariness and demoralization, Alexander and his men bluffed their way into the fortress and fell upon the count without warning. Outnumbered, the companions suffered losses, and Alexander himself engaged the count to avenge his friend Calcedor. After a fierce fight, the count fled to his tower where he was pursued by Alexander and some of his men. Others held the gateway to prevent reinforcements reaching the count.

Finally, the traitorous Count Angres was captured, but those outside the fortress did not know of Alexander's exploits. Finding his shield and those of his close companions, they thought their friends were dead. While they were mourning, prisoners from the fortress began presenting themselves, saying how Alexander had taken the town and had threatened to kill anyone who did not immediately go to King Arthur and offer their surrender.

Alexander was well rewarded by the king, and perhaps more so by Queen Guinevere, who brought Alexander and Soredamors together and pointed out to them that everyone could see they were in love. They were married, and soon had a child they named Cligès. In the meantime, messengers were sent to bring Alexander home, as his father the emperor was dying. The messengers' ship was lost in a storm, and the only survivor returned home claiming that Alexander had been killed en route. Thus his younger brother Alis became emperor.

Taking with him only a small escort, Alexander returned to Athens to confront his brother. After some negotiation they agreed that Alis would remain emperor in name, but Alexander

ABOVE: Wearing an interesting mix of armour types, Arthur rallies his troops. His high saddle is designed to help him keep his seat during the shock of a lance impact – given or received.

would hold the real power and Cligès would inherit his realm. The arrangement worked, but eventually Alexander became gravely ill. Summoning Cligès, he told the young man that he must go to Arthur's court and prove himself among the best knights in the world.

Alexander died of his illness soon after, and Soredamors from a broken heart. Part of the deal between Alexander and Alis was that the latter would not marry or produce an heir, but eventually he arranged a marriage to Fenice, daughter of the Emperor of Germany.

Magic Potions

This proposed union brought about conflict with the Duke of Saxony, to whom Fenice had been promised in marriage. Cligès led a force that defeated the Saxons, gaining the admiration of Fenice, and the two fell in love. Fenice gained the assistance of Thessala, a woman who knew how to make magical potions. The two concocted a plot whereby Alis would be given a potion that prevented him desiring Fenice, or any other woman, except in his sleep.

Cligès was tricked into giving his uncle the potion, which had its desired effect. Thus Fenice married Alis, but saved herself for Cligès. However, the Duke of Saxony planned to attack the Greeks on their return journey to Athens. Unaware of the threat, Cligès was practicing with his lance with some companions when he was ambushed by the duke's nephew. Cligès had already beaten the nephew in his previous battle against the Saxons, and now killed him with a lance thrust. Pursuing the nephew's escorts, Cligès came upon the Saxon army.

The Duke of Saxony had offered a reward to anyone who could take Cligès' head, and a knight attempted to do so. Cligès killed him and took his helm and shield, for he had none of his own with him. As he approached his army he was mistaken for an enemy, which suited him well. Cligès led his own force, now pursuing him, towards the Saxons. The Saxons thought he was their knight returning with Cligès' head, until he single-handedly attacked their host. This brought about a general engagement in which Cligès tried to capture the Duke of Saxony, but had to settle for his horse.

Meanwhile, a party of Saxon knights had captured Fenice and carried her off. A truce was declared between the warring forces, but Cligès ignored it and went after the 12 knights conveying Fenice to the Duke of Saxony. At first they thought it was their duke approaching – his horse was quite distinctive – but the truth emerged when Cligès attacked them. Six of the Saxon knights engaged Cligès – singly, of course, as custom required, and each was defeated in turn.

Cligès then fell upon the last six, slaying two with a single lance thrust. The other four were defeated with the sword, although Cligès let one go to tell the duke who had routed his men and taken back Fenice. The duke, furious, issued a personal challenge to Cligès, who was granted permission to accept. The two unhorsed one another in the first charge, then set about one another with swords in another of Chrétien de Troyes' graphic fight scenes. The exhausted Duke of Saxony proposed an honourable truce after a long fight, which Cligès accepted. The Saxons departed and the Greeks were free to return to Athens. Cligès wanted to go to Britain to join Arthur's court, but his uncle Alis would not at first grant permission. Eventually he relented and gave Cligès riches to take with him.

While Cligès was in Britain, Fenice was greatly tormented by her love for him. For his part, he obtained three sets of arms in different colours to those he already possessed, and went to take part in a tournament being held by King Arthur. The opposing team included Sagremor the Wild, who was so fearsome that none would engage him. Naturally, Cligès went straight at Sagremor, unhorsed him and took him prisoner.

Throughout the tournament Cligès took so many prisoners and fought so well that those

BELOW: This thirteenth-century illustration shows Cligès and Fenice, as well as Tristan and Isolde. The story of Cligès has been described as a satire on the 'adultery ennobled and admired' of Tristan.

he defeated gained more honour just for having faced him than many who won other fights. On that first day he wore armour all of black, but that night he concealed it, and the next morning presented himself in arms all of green. His prisoners of the first day tried to find him but could not.

This green knight was even more impressive than the black one of the day before. His first deed was to unhorse and capture Sir Lancelot, and after this he took twice as many prisoners as on the first day. Again he concealed the arms he had worn that day, appearing in red for the third day of the tourney. His notable opponent that day was Sir Perceval of Wales, who was duly captured along with many other knights.

Cligès then switched to white arms, but displayed all the others he had worn – the three incredible knights of the tourney were revealed as the same man. Sir Gawain then decided to try his skills against Cligès, and after unhorsing one another, the two battled with swords until their armour was rent and torn. Arthur himself stopped their fight and asked the two to be friends.

THE TALE OF TRISTAN AND ISEULT WAS NOT ORIGINALLY PART OF THE ARTHURIAN MYTHOS.

Cligès was invited to the court, where he revealed his identity and was warmly received. He accompanied Arthur on his progress around the realm before returning home. He and Fenice concealed their love for one another as best they could, and at one point in the tale Cligès makes reference to the story of Tristan and Iseult. This tragic tale of adultery and doomed romance was not originally part of the Arthurian mythos, but it was known at the time that Cligès' story was written. His reference to it is an oblique way of saying that Cligès does not intend to betray his uncle's marriage to Fenice.

Despite this, Fenice and Cligès plotted to leave the court of Alis together, perhaps to go to Britain. They decided to fake the death of Fenice, who feigned a long illness. With the aid of a potion made by her nurse Thessala, Fenice appeared to be dead. Despite setbacks, the deception worked well enough that Fenice and Cligès were able to live together in peace for over a year.

The two were eventually discovered and forced to flee to the court of King Arthur, who promised aid to Cligès if he warred against his uncle Alis. However, news soon came that Alis had gone mad when he could not find Cligès and Fenice, and was now dead. Cligès returned home to become emperor, taking Fenice to be his empress.

The driving force in this tale is again romance, with the reign of King Arthur as a backdrop to the adventures of Alexander and Cligès. In passing, much is revealed about the greatest knights of Arthur's realm, although they seem a little less fearsome in this tale than in their own.

Yvain, Knight of the Lion

The story of Yvain begins at a feast held by King Arthur in Carduel, Wales, at Pentecost. A group of knights, including such

BELOW: **A High Medieval depiction of various scenes involving Sir Lancelot, naturally including a tournament scene. He appears to be under suspicion; a furtive head peeks around the door to eavesdrop.**

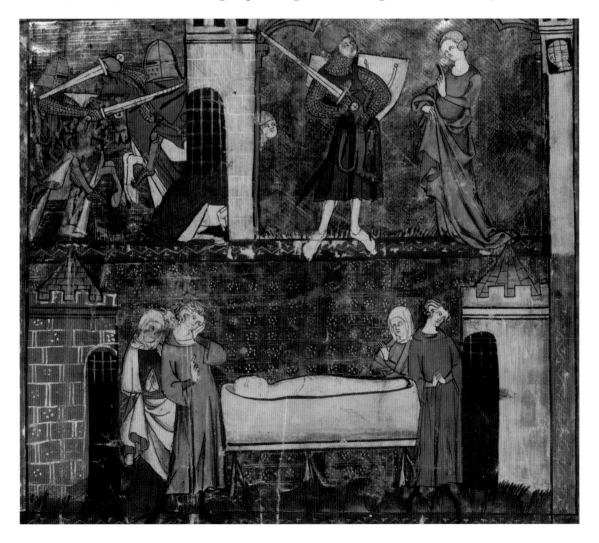

notables as Kay, Sagremor and Gawain as well as Yvain, were listening to another, Calogrenant, relating a tale and they failed to notice the approach of Queen Guinevere. Calogrenant was the only one to stand up respectfully at her approach, as custom required, earning him an angry outburst from Kay, who was annoyed at being made to seem lacking in respect.

The queen then scolded Kay for his harsh words – in this tale Kay is noted as being quarrelsome and abusive to his fellows – and an argument broke out in which Calogrenant not-very-obliquely insulted Kay and Kay returned the favour. The queen told Calogrenant to continue with his tale and not take any notice of Kay, who was so often needlessly mean that nobody took any notice.

Calogrenant then reluctantly told his tale of how seven years before he had come upon a tower in the vicinity of the forest of Brocéliande. The master of the tower received him courteously

BELOW: **The tale of Sir Yvain involves a magical stone which, when wet with water from the basin nearby, causes terrible storms. There is no explanation for how or why this happens in the tale; it is merely a plot device.**

and requested that he return later if his adventures permitted it, and the next morning Yvain rode onwards and encountered a group of bulls fighting among themselves. Watching them was a giant, 17 feet tall, who claimed that he was tending the bulls as cattle.

The giant told Calogrenant how he controlled the bulls, and in return asked his business. Yvain stated that he was in search of an adventure to test his prowess, but the giant said he had no idea where Yvain might find one. He did give him directions, however, which led him to a magical stone that could summon storms. Calogrenant went to the stone and sprinkled water upon it as he had been told, and a terrible storm immediately struck the forest.

THE STRANGE KNIGHT KNOCKED CALOGRENANT OFF HIS HORSE AND TOOK IT AS A PRIZE.

Soon after the storm subsided, Calogrenant was approached by a mysterious knight, who was extremely angry at the destruction caused by the storm. After a dramatic speech in which he spelled out the reason for his quarrel, the strange knight attacked Calogrenant, knocking him off his horse at the first pass. The knight left Calogrenant where he was, but took his horse as a prize. Returning to the tower in defeat, Calogrenant was courteously received by its lord, who told him that he was the first to return from the magical stone – all others had been killed or taken prisoner.

Yvain, who was a cousin to Calogrenant, resolved to go to the mystical rock and avenge the defeat inflicted there. However, when King Arthur heard the tale he declared that he would go there and see this wonder. He extended his invitation to any who would accompany him. This displeased Yvain, who was worried that someone else might defeat the strange knight, so he set off alone as soon as he was able.

Yvain followed his cousin's directions and found the tower where he, too, was courteously received. Passing the giant and his bulls, Yvain made his way to the magical stone and poured water on it from the golden basin that hung nearby. A storm blew up immediately, and afterwards the strange knight approached. There was no exchange of challenges this time; the two knights charged straight at one another with their lances.

When the lances were broken, the fight continued on horseback with swords. Chrétien de Troyes is careful to mention that however heated the exchange and whatever hate the two had for one another, neither struck at the other's horse as this would be considered a dishonourable act. Finally, Yvain split the knight's helm and his skull as well, giving him a mortal wound. The knight fled to his town with Yvain in pursuit.

There was no one abroad in the town, and Yvain pursued the strange knight through the gate of his fortress. This was booby-trapped, causing a portcullis to fall on Yvain and cut his horse in two, but he was so close to his quarry that he escaped injury. A second portcullis trapped Yvain, and the knight escaped beyond it.

Yvain was then met by a maiden (her name is revealed much later in the tale to be Lunete) who served the knight's lady. He spoke courteously to her, as was proper, and she told him that the entire populace were enraged at him for having dealt a mortal wound to their lord. Lunete said that she had once been sent on an errand to the court of King Arthur but no-one had deigned to speak to her. In return for his courtesy she would help Yvain escape.

The Power of Invisibility

Lunete gave Yvain a ring that made him invisible, and she brought him food and drink. While he had his meal he observed the knights of the town searching vainly for him, intent on vengeance for their lord. They even searched the room where he sat, but could not see him. The

ABOVE: A depiction of
the moment when Yvain
became trapped. The
descending portcullis
chopped his horse in two
and would have killed
him had he not been so
closely in pursuit of his
opponent.

body of the knight Yvain had killed was brought to the room,
accompanied by his beautiful wife. The knight's wounds began to
bleed, which was taken as a sign that his slayer was nearby. Yet
despite another search, no one could find Yvain.

Yvain watched the funeral procession for the knight he had
slain and wondered what to do. He needed proof that he had
killed the knight who defeated Calogrenant, which would not be
possible if he were buried. He was also greatly enamoured of the
dead knight's wife, whose name was Laudine, and he wished to
see more of her. Thus he did not flee when he had the chance,
but remained in the town, even though the entire populace was
searching for him, intent on violence.

Lunete went to Laudine, who was
still beside herself with grief. She
pointed out that there was no lord to
protect the region when King Arthur
arrived with his court, and that the
lady needed to find another husband. Her own knights were
singularly pathetic, and no match for any of Arthur's. Laudine
was eventually persuaded that the knight who bested her
husband must have been better than he, and so was deserving of
her affections.

Laudine asked who the knight was, and was informed that he
was Sir Yvain, son of King Urien. In due course, he was presented

YVAIN PRESENTED HIMSELF TO LAUDINE AND PLACED HIS FATE IN HER HANDS.

to her, and placed his fate in her hands. After some deliberation, she decided that he was a worthy husband and that they would marry very soon. Yvain was also accepted by the knights and soldiers of the town.

Thus Yvain was married to Laudine, widow of the knight he had slain. Meanwhile, Arthur's party was approaching the magical stone. Sir Kay was spouting more of his usual poison, insinuating that Yvain was a coward who had run off rather than avenge his cousin's defeat as he said he would, when Arthur poured water on the stone and caused another storm.

SIR KAY INSINUATED THAT YVAIN WAS A COWARD WHO HAD RUN OFF RATHER THAN AVENGE HIS COUSIN'S DEFEAT.

Yvain came to defend the stone, and Sir Kay requested that he be the one to fight him. At their first clash Kay was flung from the saddle and knocked unconscious. Yvain did not make him prisoner, but instead took his horse and immediately gifted it to King Arthur. When he revealed his identity, Sir Kay was humbled, which amused his companions.

Yvain invited Arthur and his party to his town, holding a feast in their honour. Sir Gawain became enamoured of Lunete, partly because she had saved his friend from the vengeance of

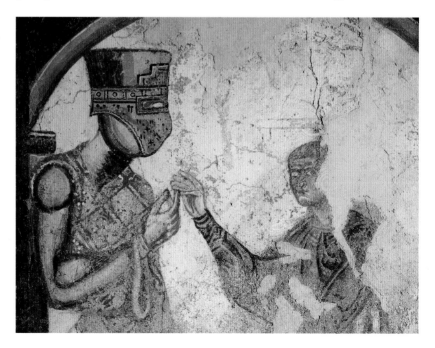

RIGHT: In this thirteenth-century fresco, Lunete provides Yvain with a magical ring that made him invisible, enabling him to avoid a lynching by the townsfolk. The story does not say where the ring came from or why she had it.

the townsfolk, and he engaged in games of courtly love with
her. However, when it was time for Arthur's party to move on,
Gawain persuaded Yvain to go with them. He warned Yvain
against becoming too complacent in marriage and forgetting his
martial virtues. Yvain told Laudine of his intentions, and asked
her permission to go seeking adventure. She agreed, on the
condition that he must return home within one year. Yvain went
off with Gawain to compete in many tournaments, winning glory
and honour. However, he forgot the passage of time. It was more
than a year later, when the king held court at Chester, that a
messenger came to the camp of the king from Laudine. Everyone
there was greeted honourably except Yvain, who was denounced
as an oathbreaker and a liar.

Laudine's messenger told Yvain that Laudine no longer loved
him and that he was unwelcome at her home. Such was his grief
that he went mad and ran off to live as a wild man in the forest
for a time. He came upon the home of a hermit who, although
frightened, fed him. Yvain repaid the hermit by hunting for
meat and bringing it to him, and for a time the two supported
one another.

Yvain was eventually found by a lady of the court and
recognized as he lay sleeping. Using a magical ointment to heal

LEFT: Yvain's opponent,
the guardian of the
magical stone, is named
Esclados, Aschelon or
some variant in different
versions of the tale. He
was merely trying to
prevent passers-by from
wrecking his town with
magical storms.

OPPOSITE: **Yvain's decision to help the lion against the dragon was a good one. The beast became a loyal friend and in turn rescued him from great danger.**

ABOVE: **Yvain did not take Laudine's rejection well. After a period of living as a wild man in the forest, he was rescued and restored to sanity by a kind damsel who used a magical ointment.**

his madness, she left gifts for him when he awoke, and soon he returned to the civilized world. The lady cared for him while his body healed, and furnished him with arms. When the town was attacked by Count Alier, seeking plunder, Yvain was armed and ready to resist him. His example – and the swift way he demolished Count Alier's knights – inspired the townsfolk to defend themselves, and the attack was beaten off.

Chrétien de Troyes describes how the count was taken prisoner, removing his helm and laying down his shield as tokens of surrender, before giving up his sword. As in other tales, even though the count is a villain who plunders towns to enrich himself, when beaten he keeps his word to live in peace with his neighbours.

Yvain then took his leave and wandered aimlessly until he came upon a lion fighting a serpent. He decided to help the lion, reasoning that serpents are always treacherous and bad. This one also spat fire, but Yvain was able to chop it into pieces. He also cut off a small part of the lion's tail to free it from the serpent's grasp.

The lion considered this acceptable and had no quarrel with his saviour. Indeed, he became a close companion of Yvain and accompanied him on his adventures. These took him to the mystical stone once again, where Yvain suffered another fit of grief-stricken madness, during which he accidentally fell on his own sword. The lion thought him dead and attempted his own suicide, throwing himself on Yvain's sword. He was prevented when Yvain recovered consciousness.

While he was bemoaning his plight, Yvain became aware of a maiden who was in a chapel nearby. She was due to be put to death for treason, and, upon asking her why, he discovered that it was Lunete. She had been accused of plotting against her mistress

traut lespee et met lescu denant son pis pour
le feu qle mal ne li face et va querre la serpent eli donne si grant coup qle li fant pla
traue entre deux oreilles.

t eil grette feu e flambe si qle li art
tout son escu e son haubert par denat
et li enst encore plus mal fait et
eil fu bistes et legiere et Recut le feu aussi
comme de tison siqne la flambe ne le Recut
me adroit et pour ce fu le feu mains ausca
et quant il voit ce si est auques effree pour
le feu dont il se doubte moult qle ne soit
enuenimes. Et toutes noires ranenne sur

Laudine, and would be put to death if she could not find a knight willing to fight in her defence against three others.

Gawain might have done so, but he was at that time busy rescuing the queen from a knight named Meleagant who had carried her off, so Lunete seemed to be doomed. Yvain promised to fight for her, but needed to find shelter for the night. In his search he came upon the fortified town of a baron who was greatly troubled by a giant. The giant wanted the baron's daughter and had killed two of his six sons who had come out to fight him. The other four were the giant's prisoners and were to be put to death in a gruesome manner if the baron did not hand over his daughter.

Yvain the Giant Slayer

Again, Yvain was told that Gawain would have assisted, but was too busy rescuing the queen. He agreed to help, providing he could complete his giant-slaying early enough in the day to save Lunete as well. The next morning, the giant brought his captive knights before the baron's walls to execute them, and Yvain rode out to fight him. Although sorely knocked about, Yvain was assisted by his lion and managed to kill the giant by severing his shoulder and stabbing him in the liver.

Yvain then rushed to where Lunete was about to be burned for her supposed treachery. After a great many courtly words Lunete's accusers, three knights, attacked Yvain all at once. He withstood their first charge, causing them to break their lances on his shield, and kept his intact. Aided by the prayers of onlookers and the more physical intervention of his lion, Yvain defeated the three knights. It is notable that these false accusers were willing to gang up on a single opponent – normally even villains would not do so.

With the false accusers dealt with, Lunete was saved. Yvain wanted a reconciliation with Laudine, but would not allow Lunete to reveal his identity, instead saying that he wanted to be known as the knight with the lion. Under this guise he had gained a reputation for helping women in need, and was sought

LUNETE'S ACCUSERS DISHONOURABLY ATTACKED YVAIN ALL AT ONCE.

out on behalf of a lady who was in dispute with her sister over an inheritance. On the way to aid her, he came upon a castle in which a great many maidens were imprisoned, having been sent there by their lord as ransom for his life.

Their captors were two devils, children of a human woman and an imp, who had slain several knights who came to rescue their prisoners. They served the lord of the castle, who told Yvain that he must fight them. If he won, he would marry the lord's daughter and receive the castle. Moreover, he must fight alone, his lion being shut away in a room and thus unable to help.

Yvain fought the two demon-brothers as best he could, but was greatly outmatched and battered with maces. The lion managed to escape and come to his aid, dragging one brother down and distracting the other so that Yvain could kill him. Yvain refused to marry the lord's daughter, however, and after freeing the captives, he proceeded to the court of King Arthur.

BELOW: **Yvain of the White Hands, depicted here, was originally a different character from Yvain, the knight with the lion. Some later versions of the tale, notably that of Malory, conflated the two.**

At the court, the dispute between the two sisters was to be decided by a battle between champions who had agreed to assist them. Yvain thus faced Gawain, who had agreed to champion the other sister. Both failed to recognize the other, which might have prevented the fight. The battle naturally went on for a long time, complete with attempts to beat out one another's brains with the pommels of swords and other graphic violence. In the meantime the onlookers began discussing how to reconcile the two sisters and thus prevent further injury to the two brave knights.

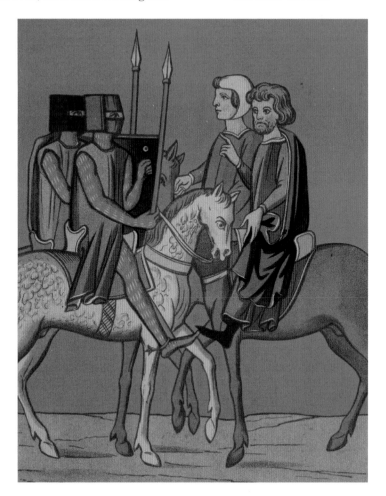

Codes of Arthurian Conduct and Honour

Yvain's legend is, like many others, driven by romance and the foolish decisions of the protagonist. Yvain becomes a knight-errant while seeking redemption for breaking his promise, a theme repeated in other Arthurian tales. Much is also made of the courtesies surrounding a fight between knights; Chrétien de Troyes describes in detail how a knight states the reasons for his quarrel before attacking. This, along with the strange contest of honour as Gawain and Yvain both try to claim defeat, illustrates the elaborate courtesies of King Arthur's era.

Finally it grew dark, and, although both knights were badly injured, neither had the advantage. Yvain finally spoke, telling Gawain how much he admired his fighting ability and asking him his identity. Gawain replied in a similarly respectful manner and said his name, at which point Yvain threw away his sword and refused to fight his friend any more. He told Gawain who he was, and conceded defeat to end the fight. Gawain would not accept, and instead offered Yvain the victory. The two then argued about who was the most battered and exhausted, each claiming defeat to give honour to his friend.

With no clear victor, the matter was passed to the king to resolve, which Arthur did. Once Yvain had recovered from his injuries, he returned to the magical stone and caused a great storm, at which point Lunete advised her lady that she must seek a new defender for the stone to prevent the town from being destroyed by storms. She said that there was none more worthy than the knight with the lion, but she knew that he could not consent to protect the town unless Laudine swore to help him reconcile himself with his lady.

Lunete brought the knight with the lion to the town, where he revealed himself to be Yvain. Trapped by her promise, Laudine was not entirely displeased, and agreed to take Yvain back when he begged forgiveness for staying away for more than the agreed year.

This tale has a number of supernatural elements – giants, magic springs and rings that make the wearer invisible, among others. Similar elements appear in earlier tales from time to time, but this is the first in which they play such a major role.

Lancelot, Knight of the Cart

Chrétien de Troyes mentioned Sir Lancelot in passing in other tales, but this is the first in which he was the central character. It is also his first mention of Camelot; indeed, probably the first mention of it anywhere. King Arthur was holding court on Ascension Day at Camelot when a strange knight arrived and

announced that he had taken several of Arthur's knights captive. The knight added that Arthur would not be able to rescue them by force of arms, but he was willing to take part in a contest with a single knight of the court for their release. That knight would have to escort the queen into a forest where the knight would be waiting, and if he managed to defend Guinevere and return to court with her, the prisoners would be released.

Sir Kay, Arthur's seneschal, then announced that he intended to leave the court, but would not say why. When begged by Queen Guinevere to remain or at least explain his reasons, Kay said that he would do so in return for a favour from the king. The favour turned out to be to entrust the queen's safety to Kay as he went to face the mysterious knight. Arthur was not pleased, but agreed to the request.

Kay and Guinevere set out for the forest, and Gawain proposed to Arthur that they follow to see how things turned

ABOVE: **A tournament scene featuring King Nabor, Sir Gawain and the Count des Broches, taken from the 1344** *Romance of Lancelot of the Lake.*

ABOVE: A typical Arthurian story: Lancelot fights a wicked knight to save a lady. The shields of those who have previously tried and failed are hung on the tree as trophies.

OPPOSITE: Guinevere is depicted here as a paragon of beauty and gentle nobility. Her part in the Arthurian legend is mostly passive, yet destructive. It was her affair with Lancelot that ultimately broke the fellowship among Arthur's knights.

out. They encountered Kay's horse running wild as they approached the forest, and soon afterwards a knight whose horse was exhausted. Gawain gave him a spare mount and he rode off, but shortly afterwards Arthur's party found the horse dead amid the wreckage caused by a fight between several knights.

They found the knight again, on foot, approaching a cart. This cart was of a sort used to drag criminals through the streets of a town, and was driven by a dwarf. The dwarf would not tell the knight if he had any news of the queen, but promised that if he got into the cart he would soon hear of her. After hesitating for a moment, the knight got into the cart, despite the disgrace associated with it.

Gawain was offered a seat in the cart but declined to accept the dishonour. Instead, he rode beside it until they came to a town. The townsfolk poured scorn upon the knight in the cart but he would not say why he was in it. Coming to a tower the two knights were courteously received and shown to fine beds, but told that another, even better, bed in the same room was not for them. The lady of the tower would not explain why this was, saying that a knight who had been in a cart had no business asking such questions. The knight of the cart then got into the bed in defiance of the lady.

During the night, a lance with a burning pennon on it descended from the ceiling and set the bed on fire, but it only wounded the knight very slightly. He put out the fire and threw the lance away, then went back to sleep. In the morning, the knights saw a bier being carried by, upon which lay a knight.

Ire chevalier fait monseigneur
gauuain car ales ius de la char
rette et montes sur ce cheval q̃
moult est bon aincoys que pl'
grant honte vous en viengue.
Dehait ait fait le nain qui ce
locita ne il nen fera riens car il ma creante q̃
il venra huy toute iour iusques au vespre sur
ma charrette et lancelot luy dist que il nait
ia garde. car il nen descendra huy mais iusq̃s
a donecque ilz saront herbagies. Certes fait
mons gauuain ce voise a moy car ie cuid que

Behind the bier came a horse ridden by the queen, led by another knight. A crowd followed them.

Gawain and the knight of the cart armed themselves and followed, but were unable to catch up. They encountered a maiden waiting at a crossroads, who offered information if they would pledge themselves to assist her when she asked. They did so, and were told that Queen Guinevere was the captive of Meleagant, a knight from the kingdom of Gorre. It was almost impossible to enter that land, she told them, except by a highly dangerous bridge that was underwater and another – even more perilous – called the sword bridge.

Gawain chose to chance the water bridge, and the knight of the cart said he would try the sword bridge. They thus parted after exchanging courtesies and good wishes. The knight of the cart, lost in thought, failed to notice a knight guarding a ford ahead of him. His thirsty horse approached it to drink, causing the knight to attack. The knight of the cart knew nothing of this until knocked from his horse by the other knight's lance. Landing in the ford, he finally became aware of the other, and asked why he was being attacked.

The knight of the ford said that his three challenges had gone unheeded, and, after some harsh words, the two agreed to joust. The fight went on for some time on foot, and during it the knight of the cart reflected bitterly on his dismal performance in his quest so far. Finally defeating the other knight, the knight of the cart took him prisoner, but was persuaded to release his captive by a damsel the knight of the ford had with him.

The knight of the cart was then approached by another damsel, who offered him hospitality on condition that he would sleep with her. The knight of the cart agreed, with strange reluctance, and the two went to her home. Despite the fact that no servants or staff could be seen around, the knight was treated courteously and ate with the damsel. Afterwards, she told him to come shortly to her chamber, but when he did he found her being attacked by a strange knight who had with him several guards.

OPPOSITE: The cart in which Lancelot rode was of a sort used to parade criminals around town. Using such a common mode of transport was bad enough, but being carried in this manner was a deep disgrace for a knight.

GUINEVERE WAS THE CAPTIVE OF MELEAGANT, A KNIGHT FROM THE KINGDOM OF GORRE.

Damsel in Distress?

The knight of the cart attempted a rescue, fighting his way through the guards despite receiving a wound, and eventually ended up with his back against the wall facing several opponents. At this point the damsel dismissed the guards, who were of her own household, and after they had gone she led the knight to her bed.

The knight of the cart wanted to keep his promise to the damsel, but was reluctant. Chrétien de Troyes makes it very clear that he is in love with someone else, although he does not say whom at this point. The damsel picked up on the knight's less than subtle cues and left him to his rest.

In the morning the damsel asked the knight of the cart to escort her on the road. The author explains that it was the custom of the time that a knight who encountered an unescorted lady was honour-bound to protect her and do her no harm, but if an escorting knight were defeated then the captor could do as he pleased with the lady without any shame or dishonour.

After a time the knight and his companion found a comb that belonged to the queen, and soon afterwards they were approached by a knight. The damsel recognized him, saying that he had been paying court to her, but that she was not interested in his advances. The knight declared that he was going to carry the damsel off, but the knight of the cart stated that she was under his escort. The two agreed to find a suitable place to fight for the damsel.

A KNIGHT WHO CAME ACROSS AN UNESCORTED LADY WAS HONOUR-BOUND TO PROTECT HER.

Coming to a meadow that might be suitable for a joust, the knights encountered a party of nobles taking their leisure there. Among them was the father of the knight who wanted to carry off the damsel. Recognizing the knight of the cart, they cursed him and would not play games or dance while he was present. Nor would they permit the fight to take place, although the father and son decided to follow the knight of the cart and judge him by his deeds.

Next, the knight of the cart came upon a chapel, which had a very beautiful cemetery. Tombs were ready, inscribed with the names of famous knights who were to lie in them, among them

LEFT: 'Sir Lancelot in the Chapel Perilous' by Walter Crane (1911). Here, Lancelot discovers tombs prepared for famous knights, including himself.

Gawain and Yvain. The greatest of the tombs had a lid that seemed too heavy even for several men to lift. The knight of the cart was told that whoever could lift it alone would set free all the prisoners in the land where all foreigners were captive.

The knight of the cart easily lifted off the lid, and a monk who observed the feat asked who he was. He would not say, but asked whose tomb it was. In return, he was told that it was the tomb of whoever freed the captives from Meleagant's homeland.

Hearing of this deed, the father and son following the knight of the cart agreed that this was a very worthy knight, even though they did not know his name. The son gave up on his intention to seek a fight, and the two turned back. The damsel also returned to her home, and the knight of the cart rode onwards.

Soon afterward, the knight of the cart met another knight who offered the hospitality of his home. There, the knight of the cart learned that his family were people of Logres who could not return home. Natives of the land where they were forced to remain could come and go as they pleased, but foreigners could never leave. Two of the knight's sons offered to show him the way to the sword bridge and to assist in fighting past any defenders. The three were offered hospitality by a man whose

RIGHT: The sword bridge was the most dangerous of the two ways into the Kingdom of Gorre. Lancelot was gravely injured in making the crossing, and had to leave behind his companions.

house lay well ahead on the road, but before they could reach it they encountered a local squire who was greatly agitated. The squire told them that the people of Logres, long imprisoned in that land, had risen up and were fighting their captors, and that a powerful knight had come to help them.

Pleased at hearing this, the three entered a fortress they encountered, but became trapped by gates that closed behind them. The knight of the cart thought that there must be sorcery at work here, and tried to use a magical ring he had that would dispel it. The ring was given to him by a fairy or a lady (the lady of the lake), depending on the version of the tale. It revealed that there was no enchantment, only mortal bars, so the three chopped their way through with their swords.

LANCELOT AND HIS COMPANIONS LED THE PEOPLE OF LOGRES TO A GREAT VICTORY OVER THEIR CAPTORS.

Once outside, the three saw a battle going on, but could not tell which side their own people were on. Once they had determined which side to join, they entered the fray and helped the people of Logres to win a great victory. Afterward they heaped praise upon the knight of the cart, almost coming to blows over who was to offer him hospitality. The knight of the cart persuaded them instead to give him lodgings best suited to his mission, and pressed on in the morning.

The following night, when the three had stopped at a nobleman's house, a strange knight confronted them and offered to convey the knight of the cart across the stream spanned by the bridge of swords. His condition was that at the other side he would choose whether or not to kill the knight of the cart. This was unacceptable, so the two fought. This joust is notable in that both knights strike at the other's mount, which is normally considered dishonourable.

The knight of the cart finally forced his opponent to surrender, and agreed to spare him on condition that he must also ride in a cart and be shamed; he had said many unpleasant things about the event before the fight began. The beaten knight refused, but before the knight of the cart could execute him a maiden arrived and asked for the defeated knight's head.

The knight of the cart pondered whether to show mercy or grant the maiden's request. He was in the habit of always granting mercy if it was asked for – which was the custom of the time – but was also driven to generously grant any request made of him that lay within his power. His solution was to fight a second time; again the knight was beaten and begged mercy, but this time he was beheaded. The maiden told the knight of the cart that he wold be rewarded in due course and went on her way.

Finally, the knight of the cart and his two companions reached the sword bridge. This took the form of a sword blade, as long as two lances, over a raging river. The two companions of the knight of the cart were fearful and would not cross, and he was wounded by the sharp bridge before he reached the other side. There, he saw a tower in whose window he saw Bademagu, king of that land, and his son Meleagant.

Bademagu, who was an honourable man, was impressed by the crossing and suggested to his son that he should surrender Queen Guinevere. Meleagant, who was anything but honourable, declined. King Bademagu offered the newcomer hospitality until his wounds were healed, but the knight of the cart would wait only until the next day, and that was out of deference to his host.

Lancelot Unveiled

The next morning Meleagant and the knight of the cart charged at one another, bringing about another of Chrétien de Troyes' fight scenes. The violence of the encounter is demonstrated in descriptions of how pieces of armour and equipment are shattered or torn asunder – bits of saddle are scattered over the field, and both knights are repeatedly wounded. Finally, the knight of the cart was worn down, weakened by his injuries from crossing the sword bridge. A clever lady asked the queen if she knew who this knight was, and his identity was finally revealed as Lancelot of the Lake. Calling to him by name, the lady let him see that Guinevere was watching.

> UNSURE OF WHETHER OR NOT TO GRANT MERCY, LANCELOT'S SOLUTION WAS TO FIGHT A SECOND TIME.

Inspired, Lancelot began to get the best of the fight, and
King Bademagu asked Guinevere to have Lancelot spare his son.
Lancelot, who would do anything for the queen, naturally did
so. Meleagant was not pleased, but agreed to a peace whereby he
would surrender Guinevere on condition that Lancelot fight him
again in a year. If he failed to do so, then the queen would have
to place herself again in captivity.

Guinevere behaved rather coldly to Lancelot at first, refusing
to speak to him. Lancelot and King Bademagu went to see Sir
Kay, Arthur's seneschal, who was wounded and in captivity along
with Guinevere. Kay told how the king had tried to treat his
wounds and his treacherous son Meleagant kept undoing
his work.

Lancelot went to meet Gawain, who had entered Bademagu's
land by the other route, and took with him many of the people
of Logres. Some remained with the queen, although they were
now free to leave. On the way Lancelot was captured by local
men, who thought they were doing their king a service, and news
reached Guinevere that Lancelot had been put
to death.

As Guinevere laments her actions towards
Lancelot, Chrétien de Troyes makes it very
clear that they were already lovers before her
abduction. This explains some of Lancelot's
earlier actions and his desperation to rescue
her. Guinevere mourned Lancelot for two days,
refusing to eat, and he heard that she had died.
He resolved to kill himself by contriving a
noose from his belt, intending to be dragged by
the neck behind his horse. He was saved from
this enterprise by his companions, and soon
afterwards heard that Guinevere was alive.

For her part, the queen was pleased to hear
that Lancelot had tried (and failed) to kill
himself upon hearing of her supposed death. When he returned
to Bademagu's castle, she explained that she was angry with him
for hesitating to enter the cart, placing the desire to avoid shame
ahead of his need to rescue her.

BELOW: Guinevere was
offended that Lancelot
had hesitated rather than
jumping straight into
the cart and accepting
the associated disgrace.
She considered her
rescue (or perhaps his
devotion to her) as
more important than
Lancelot's reputation.

RIGHT: Lancelot's furtive night-time visits to Guinevere were noticed by other members of the court. Some were sure that there was an innocent explanation, and Lancelot always offered to fight anyone who said that Guinevere was unfaithful to her husband.

That evening, Lancelot broke into Guinevere's tower to spend the night with her, injuring his hand in the process. His blood stained her bed, and the following morning Meleagant drew the obvious conclusion, for the wounded Kay was lodged nearby. Kay naturally denied the charge and offered to fight in defence of the queen's good name, even though he was still suffering greatly from his wounds.

Trial by Combat

Lancelot then offered to fight in defence of both Kay and Guinevere against Meleagant who accused them. Before the encounter, Meleagant swore upon holy relics that Kay had spent the night with the queen, and Lancelot swore (truthfully, but misleadingly) that he had not. The fight thus became a judicial duel, a trial by combat in which the winner would be assumed to have the truth of the matter.

Meleagant and Lancelot unhorsed one another in the first pass, and set about their work with swords. King Bademagu asked Guinevere to halt the fight, and she agreed, so Lancelot paused. However, Meleagant wanted to fight on and had to be stopped by his father's physical intervention. After this, Lancelot left to meet Gawain, accompanied by many of the people of Logres who wanted to return home.

On the way, they met a dwarf who persuaded Lancelot to leave his party on some secret errand. Unable to find Lancelot, his companions pressed on until they found Gawain drowning in the river after having tried to cross the water bridge. Gawain was rescued and informed that Guinevere was safe under the care of King Bademagu, and that Lancelot had tried to rescue her, but was now missing in the company of a mysterious dwarf.

Returning to King Bademagu, Gawain and others searched for Lancelot, but could not find him, even with the help of the king's men. Then a letter arrived, apparently from Lancelot, saying that he had gone home to King Arthur's court and they should all join him there. They did so, and Gawain was praised for rescuing Guinevere. No one at court had seen Lancelot, and still he could not be found.

Lancelot was at that time imprisoned in a tower by a vassal of Meleagant. He heard that a tournament was to be held in Arthur's realm, and wished to attend it. The wife of his captor was persuaded to let him go on condition that he return and become a prisoner again afterwards, thus sparing her household the wrath of Meleagant.

Lancelot attended the tournament incognito. However, he was recognized by a herald, who proclaimed that one had come who would take the measure but would not reveal his identity.

Although there were many skilled knights in the tourney, Lancelot defeated everyone who stood against him until Queen Guinevere sent him a message asking him to do his worst. He immediately began to miss his lance thrusts and to flee from other knights, becoming a figure of ridicule in the process.

Seeing the mysterious knight fighting so badly at her request, Guinevere knew it was Lancelot. On the second day of the tournament Guinevere again sent a message to Lancelot to do his worst, and he agreed to do whatever she asked of him. Certain of his identity, she then requested that he perform at his best. Lancelot did so, unhorsing many knights – one by a hundred feet – and giving away the horses he won from them. At the end of the day he slipped away and returned to his prison.

LANCELOT HIT A KNIGHT SO HARD THAT HE FLEW ONE HUNDRED FEET OUT OF THE SADDLE.

Meleagant had Lancelot walled up in a tower after this, and went to the court of King Arthur. There, he announced that he had come to fight Lancelot as agreed, and since Lancelot had not presented himself, the duel could not take place. Meleagant graciously allowed Lancelot a year to make his appearance and agreed that if he did not, Gawain would fight in his place.

Meleagant then went home and told his father what he had done. King Bademagu was not impressed, and more importantly his daughter overheard and resolved to find Lancelot. After much searching she found the tower where Lancelot was lamenting the fact that Gawain had not come to rescue him.

The lady revealed that it was she who had asked Lancelot for the head of a knight she hated, and since he had obliged her she would now repay the favour by getting him out of the tower. He was weak from his long confinement, so she took care of him until he was ready to return home. He arrived just as Meleagant was about to fight Gawain in Lancelot's stead.

Gawain offered to fight Meleagant anyway, but Lancelot would have none of it. He and Meleagant charged with lances, and even after they were both unhorsed they fought one another on foot. Lancelot severed Meleagant's arm and smashed in his teeth before finally beheading him.

This tale ends rather abruptly with Lancelot's victory over his enemy. It takes place at roughly the same time as the story of Yvain; that tale refers now and then to Gawain and Lancelot being away from court rescuing the queen, and Lancelot being detained in the tower. The stories of Yvain and Gawain establish a number of characters and key concepts in the Arthurian legends, which are built upon by later writers.

ABOVE: Lancelot was permitted to leave captivity in order to fight in a tournament. Nobody but Guinevere seems to have suspected that the knight demolishing all comers was Lancelot in disguise.

Arguably, these two romances belong to the 'developed' Arthur myth, whereas Chrétien de Troyes' first two tales fall somewhere between the original tale and the mature version. This makes sense; the author was creating his mythos as he wrote his tales. The later ones naturally have a more developed background.

An increasing amount of religious and supernatural elements enter the mythos in the works of Chrétien de Troyes. There are a couple of monsters in the Geoffrey of Monmouth version, but by the time Gawain and Lancelot begin their adventures the world seems to be rife with them.

There are, however, less supernatural elements to Lancelot's tale than Yvain's. The magical ring Lancelot has is singularly unimpressive, and there are no giants or supernatural beasts. There is something otherworldly about Bademagu's realm, however, with its strange bridges and ability to trap foreigners so that they cannot leave. The main thrust of the story is, of course, the adulterous affair between Lancelot and Guinevere that, it is clear, had been going on for some time before the tale began.

THE GRAIL QUEST

The quest for the Holy Grail is one of the central tales of the Arthurian mythos, and its development is a complex one. The earliest Grail story was written – but left unfinished – by Chrétien de Troyes around 1180. This was the tale of Perceval, the original Grail hero.

Later versions of the story finished it and added more content, as well as relegating Perceval to a supporting role. Perceval's father varies, depending on the version of the tale. In some variants, he was the son of King Pellinore of the Isles. Perceval was raised without knowledge of courtly ways, but as a young man he saw a group of knights and wanted to be like them. Journeying to the court of King Arthur, he was inducted into the fellowship of the Round Table.

In the early version of the Grail story, Perceval encountered the Fisher King, Guardian of the Grail. The Fisher King was badly wounded – most versions of the tale say his injury was in

OPPOSITE: This 1912 painting is a classic representation of the questing knight; in this case it is Parsifal (Perceval). The Grail Quest was the beginning of the end for Round Table fellowship.

ABOVE: Illustrations from the original Chrétien de Troyes version of the Grail Quest, featuring events from the life of Perceval. Later authors relegated him to a supporting role and introduced the saintly Galahad as the Grail Hero.

the thigh, but this was a common euphemism for a wound to the genitals – and could do little more than fish in the river outside his castle.

The Grail and the Lance

The Fisher King was kept alive by the power of the Grail, but could not be healed until a perfect knight used the bleeding lance. In the original tales, the Grail and the lance were apparently not connected with Christianity; the lance is described as poisonous and the Grail is not explicitly holy. Later versions of the story made the Grail the cup of Christ; the lance became the spear that pierced him while he hung on the cross. There are also versions of the tale in which there are two Grail kings, both wounded.

In the meantime, the Fisher King's realm of Listerneise had become the Wasteland, ever since he was struck down by a blow called the Dolorous Stroke. The land would be healed when its king was, but when Perceval first visited the Fisher King's castle he was too ignorant of courtly ways to carry out the task. Dining with the Fisher King, Perceval watched a procession consisting of a candelabra, the bleeding lance and the Grail take place between each course of the meal, but he did not ask about their significance.

Perceval thus did not learn how to heal the Fisher King, and when he woke the next day the castle was a ruin. He vowed to find the Grail castle again, but whether or not he would have remains unknown; Chrétien de Troyes died before completing the tale.

In 1210 Wolfram von Eschenbach wrote a version of the tale entitled *Parzival*. This generally followed the earlier story with a few variations. Among them was the statement that the Fisher King's wound was a punishment for his failure to remain chaste.

Further versions of the tale were incorporated into what has become known as the Lancelot-Grail cycle. This includes a history of the Holy Grail and how it came to be in England, and a description of the life and times of Merlin. Lancelot's adventures are the main focus, of course, and among them is an incident where he was tricked into sleeping with Elaine, daughter of the Fisher King. Lancelot thought he was visiting Guinevere, and from this union came Galahad.

Galahad is a later addition to the story, supplanting Perceval as the Grail knight. Perceval remains important, but as a companion to Galahad rather than the protagonist of the story. The Lancelot-Grail cycle tells of Galahad's completion of the Grail Quest and of the death of Arthur.

More is made of the religious significance of events in this later version, and indeed Galahad is presented almost as a 'lesser Christ' whose piety and perfection shows up the flaws and shortcomings of the other Round Table Knights. They are still chivalrous heroes, but of all of them only two – Perceval and Bors – are good enough to accompany Galahad, and only he can complete the Grail Quest.

The following version of the Grail Quest dates from around 1210. As noted above, earlier variants would have had Perceval as the hero, and many incidents would have lesser significance or be omitted entirely.

ABOVE: Galahad, Perceval and Bors were the only knights holy enough to complete the Grail Quest. All others failed due to a lack of piety and chastity, or through various worldly sins.

The Grail Quest Begins

The story of the Grail Quest began at the feast of Pentecost, when the Knights of the Round Table were gathered at Camelot. A lady arrived, searching for Lancelot, and asked that he accompany her to the forest. As seems to be the way of these things, she would not say what the errand was, but merely indicated that all would soon become clear.

The damsel led Lancelot to a nunnery where he found his cousins Bors and Lyonel. He was also introduced to a youth named Galahad, who hoped to become a knight. Lancelot agreed to knight him, which was normal at the time the tale was written. Until the 1500s, any knight could elevate another to knighthood; after this it became a royal prerogative only. Galahad would not accompany the others to Camelot, however.

When they returned to court, Lancelot and his kinsmen discussed Galahad, wondering if he was related to them. They

THE SWORD IN THE STONE

The Knights of the Round Table had a custom that they would not sit down to eat on a high feast day until some adventure or notable happening had occurred. This took the form of a stone floating in the river, through which a sword was pierced. The sword bore an inscription that stated it could only be drawn from the stone by the knight who was to wield it – the best knight in all creation.

Arthur suggested that Lancelot should have the sword, since he was the best of them, but Lancelot refused to touch it. He stated that anyone who tried and failed to draw the sword from the stone would receive a wound from it, adding that the adventure of the Holy Grail would begin that day. Gawain and Perceval tried to draw the sword, but could not, but the events of the day were sufficiently wondrous that dinner could now be served.

RIGHT: Gawain tried (and failed) to remove the sword from the stone. Later, he did indeed receive a blow from the sword – it was in the hand of Galahad at the time – just as Lancelot had predicted.

then read the names on the seats around the Round Table. Each was inscribed with the name of the knight who was to sit there. One, named the Perilous Seat, had mysteriously gained a new inscription, which said that on Pentecost in the year 454 AD it would be filled – that very day. They covered the words with a cloth. The only empty chair at the Round Table was the Perilous Seat, and during dinner a white-robed man appeared, leading by the hand a knight in scarlet armour who had no sword or shield. The latter was introduced as the Knight Desired, a descendant of Joseph of Arimathea.

The white-robed man led the knight to the Perilous Seat, and removing the cloth, revealed that the words inscribed there had mysteriously changed. They now said that this was the seat of Galahad, nephew of King Pelles and grandson of the Fisher King. The white-robed man left, and Galahad joined the company of the Round Table.

At this point the author implies a backstory to the Perilous Seat, saying that worthy men had feared it and it had been the cause of many adventures. He does not explain any of this, merely referring to it in passing. The Perilous Seat had apparently caused misfortune to befall anyone who tried to sit in it, and was seen as a test that showed Galahad to be a very worthy knight. He also reveals that Galahad is the son of Lancelot by the daughter of the Fisher King.

Galahad explained that he had come to Camelot because it was time for the Grail Quest to begin. In the meantime, the knights showed Galahad the mysterious sword-pierced stone. Galahad was not surprised that no-one else could pull the sword

ABOVE: **The Perilous Seat – sometimes called the Siege Perilous – caused disaster and death for anyone unworthy who sat in it. When Galahad took his place there, everyone knew that something wondrous was occurring.**

out; he had known he was to receive this weapon and thus had brought no sword with him when he came to court. Once he had pulled out the sword and buckled it on, King Arthur said that he would presumably soon be sent a shield by some equally marvellous process.

At this juncture a maiden rode up and informed Lancelot that he must no longer consider himself the best knight in the world. She added that Nascien the Hermit sent word that the Holy Grail would that day appear in Camelot. Naturally, this was grounds for a tournament, which must be a particularly spectacular event since Arthur was sure some of the knights would not survive their coming adventure.

Galahad refused all offers of a shield, but nevertheless excelled in the tourney. He defeated all the companions of the Round Table except Lancelot and Perceval. Afterwards the company went to dinner, and as predicted the Holy Grail appeared. No-one could see who was carrying the Grail, but where it passed plates were filled with the favourite foods of those who sat at the tables.

Gawain was the first to pledge that the following day he would embark upon the quest of the Holy Grail, and after him all the other knights also swore to do so. All promised to search until they once again witnessed the grail, which worried Arthur. He knew that many would not come back from this endeavour, either due to its perils or a reluctance to give up the quest once started.

GAWAIN WAS THE FIRST TO SWEAR THAT HE WOULD UNDERTAKE THE GRAIL QUEST.

After dinner another mysterious visitor arrived, this time an old man in religious clothing. He said that Nascien the Hermit sent word that the Grail Quest was a holy endeavour, to be undertaken only by pious men who had confessed and been absolved of their sins.

After swearing great oaths on sacred relics the knights rode out on their quest. Arthur rode with them for a time, until Gawain told him he must return to Camelot. He did so, and soon afterwards the companions came to the castle of Vagan. Vagan had been a great knight in his youth, and was determined to show the companions hospitality even if it meant closing the gates of his castle to prevent them leaving.

Galahad's Shield

The next morning, the companions separated and began their quest in earnest. Galahad travelled for a few days before reaching an abbey where he found Yvain and King Bademagus, both Knights of the Round Table. They told him that they had come to the abbey after hearing of a shield that was kept there. No knight could use it without meeting some dreadful misfortune. Yvain would not chance it, but Bademagus was determined to try. They agreed that since Galahad did not have a shield of his own he should take this one if Bademagus failed.

ABOVE: Galahad arrives at one of the many abbeys he visits in his adventure. The White Friars feature prominently in this tale, offering praise and guidance to the worthy, and delivering several stern lectures about sin to Lancelot.

Bademagus took up the shield but had not ridden far when he was assailed by a knight in white armour, who wounded and unhorsed him with ease. The white knight chided Bademagus for taking the shield and gave it to a squire to take to Galahad. He then accompanied the squire and Bademagus, who was badly wounded and expected to die, to the abbey. The monks said that he might survive, but in any case was not to be much pitied as he had been warned about the foolishness of taking the shield.

The white knight told Galahad that the shield was that of Joseph of Arimathea, who had taken Jesus down from the cross. By way of many adventures it had come to this place to wait for the knight who was to bear it next. Hearing this, the squire begged Galahad to make him a knight and allow him to join the quest, which he granted. They went back to the abbey to obtain

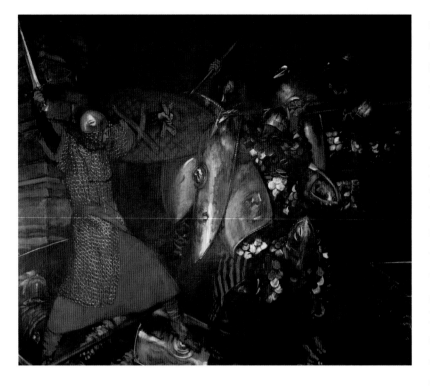

ABOVE: Galahad defeated seven wicked knights, but let them flee rather than slaying them. This mattered little, as they soon ran into Gawain and his companions. All seven were killed.

arms for the squire, and were there told of a strange voice that issued from one of the tombs in the cemetery.

In the tomb was the body of a wicked knight whose spirit was driven away by Galahad's piety. Galahad was informed that this adventure was a metaphor for the coming of Christ into a hard and pitiless world, and that Galahad's coming quest was of a similar nature. He would find the causes of many misfortunes afflicting the world and remove them.

The next morning, Galahad – although himself a knight for less than a week – knighted the squire. His name was Melyant, and his father was the King of Denmark. Melyant asked to come with Galahad on his quest, and Galahad agreed. They journeyed together for a time until they came to a parting of the road. The left path was said to be very perilous, and only the best of knights should take it. Galahad had a mind to, but Melyant asked to be permitted to go, as he wished to test himself.

Melyant had not gone far when he found a crown lying on a seat in the path. He took it, and was then approached by a knight who said he should not have done so. The two charged at one another, and Melyant was gravely wounded. As he lay helpless, Galahad rode up. They both agreed that the wound was likely mortal, but before anything could be done Galahad in turn was attacked by the strange knight.

Galahad broke his lance defeating this first knight, but defended himself with this shield against the charge of a second. He cut off this knight's hand with his sword and let him flee while he helped Melyant to a nearby abbey. The monks there said they could heal Melyant in a month or so, and Galahad stated that he would continue the quest alone. Hearing that the two were engaged upon the Grail Quest, the monks told Melyant that he had been wounded because of his sins.

Melyant's first sin was of pride, thinking that he was worthy enough to chance the left-hand path, and his second was to covet the crown he found upon it. He had avoided death only due to his faith in God, who had spared him so that he might learn from the mistakes at a future time, and would trust in the Lord rather than his own powers. Galahad, who was without sin, had easily withstood the attack of both knights and defeated them.

GALAHAD, WHO WAS WITHOUT SIN, EASILY WITHSTOOD THE ASSAULT OF THE TWO KNIGHTS.

Galahad left Melyant at the abbey and rode on until he came to a ruined chapel. Praying there, he heard a voice telling him to go to the Maidens' castle and defeat the evil he found there. A man he met on the road told him that the Maidens' castle was cursed. He rode there and was confronted by seven knights who attacked him all at once. However, they did declare their intent first and said that this was the practice at their castle.

Galahad's battle with the seven knights went on for hours, and they grew weary, although he did not. When the seven fled from him he did not pursue and was soon after approached by an old man, who gave him the keys to the castle. Within its walls were many damsels who were pleased at their deliverance, but feared that the seven knights would simply come back after Galahad left.

BELOW: Galahad was given the keys to the castle, and provided for its protection by making the local nobles swear to defend it. He then gifted the castle back to its rightful owner and continued his quest.

The old man explained that the seven knights had taken the castle and the lands surrounding it from Duke Lynor, who they had killed. It was prophesied that they would lose the castle because of a damsel, so they imprisoned every lady who passed by. This was the origin of the castle's name.

The knights and lords of the surrounding lands were summoned by Galahad, who made them swear not to permit a return to the custom of imprisoning passing maidens. He granted the castle back to the surviving daughter of Duke Lynor. The seven brothers, meanwhile, had encountered Gawain, Yvain and Gawain's brother Gaheriet, and were now dead.

The Sins of Gawain and Lancelot

Gawain, in the meantime, had come to the abbey where Melyant lay wounded, and asked where Galahad had gone. The friars told him that he was not suitable to accompany Galahad, since Gawain was a wicked man and Galahad was much better than he. They would not say why they thought this, but told Gawain that he would soon meet someone who could tell him.

Soon after, a knight arrived at the abbey. This was Gawain's brother Gaheriet, and together they rode until they met Yvain on the road. After encountering (and killing) the seven brothers defeated by Galahad, they took a different route and did not meet him. Instead, they met a hermit who was very holy, and Gawain made confession to him. This was his first confession in four years. The hermit told Gawain that this was why he had been called wicked by the friars, and that if he had led a more pious life he might have shown the seven brothers a better path rather than simply killing them.

GAWAIN MIGHT HAVE REDEEMED THE SEVEN BROTHERS IF HE WAS NOT SUCH A TERRIBLE SINNER HIMSELF.

The hermit also explained that the seven brothers represented the seven great sins, and the imprisonment of the damsels was a metaphor for the fact that souls were imprisoned in hell unless freed by Jesus Christ. Galahad's rescue of the damsels was thus another parallel between his quest for the Holy Grail and the coming of Christ. Gawain was urged to do penance for his wickedness, but he declined.

Galahad, meanwhile, rode on and encountered Perceval and Lancelot. They failed to recognize him, as they did not know about the shield he had been given, and attacked him. Galahad unhorsed Lancelot and stunned Perceval with a blow to the head. He then went into the Forest Gaste, and they followed but could not find him. Lancelot pressed on and Perceval went back to find a hermit who had said she knew the name of the knight they fought.

In the forest, Lancelot found a ruined chapel, but could not get in. As he rested nearby a sick knight approached on a litter drawn by two horses. Lancelot saw that within the chapel were a candelabra and cross, and upon a silver table stood a vessel he recognized as the Holy Grail. The knight entered the chapel and was healed, but Lancelot remained half-asleep outside. The formerly sick knight mused that Lancelot had been denied the chance to witness this great event due to his sins.

Lancelot's helm and sword, and his horse, were taken by the knight, who rode off and left him sleeping in the forest. Finally

ABOVE: **Failing to recognize Galahad, Lancelot and Perceval fought him and were quickly defeated. They parted company, with Lancelot going after Galahad and Perceval, seeking information about the knight who had defeated him.**

ABOVE: Lancelot chanced upon the Holy Grail in a chapel in the forest, but was so full of sin that he slept through a miracle there – and also got robbed of his sword and horse.

waking, Lancelot tried to enter the chapel, but was told to go away by a voice he heard, which said that his sinful presence sullied the place.

Lamenting his sins, Lancelot found a holy hermit whose parables indicated he had wasted the many gifts he had. Lancelot wanted to confess his sins, but could not at first bring himself to speak of his adultery with the queen. Finally he did so, and the hermit absolved him, so long as he promised not to repeat the sin.

Perceval sought knowledge of the knight he and Lancelot had fought, and found a hermit who turned out to be his aunt. She told him that the strange knight was one of the three knights who would complete the Grail Quest, along with Bors and Perceval himself, and that he was Galahad. Perceval's aunt also went on at some length about the importance of piety and purity.

Riding on, Perceval visited an abbey where he saw an old man with many wounds apparently come back to life during Mass. He was told that this was King Mordrain, who had fought against the enemies of Christianity in Britain 400 years previously. Mordrain had wanted to see the Holy Grail for himself and got too close – he was struck blind and helpless. He had prayed to live until the knight who would behold the Grail came, and thus remained alive but helpless, able only to eat the sacramental wafer at Mass each day. He was of course waiting for Galahad.

Pressing on, Perceval encountered an armed party bearing the body of their lord. They asked him who he was, and when he answered that he was of King Arthur's court they attacked him. His horse was killed and he was wounded, and would have been slain if the knight in scarlet armour – Galahad – had not intervened. Galahad routed the attackers then rode quickly off without speaking to Perceval, who followed on foot.

Chancing upon a valet leading a fine horse, Perceval asked to borrow it. The valet refused, since he feared the horse's owner. Dismayed that he would lose the trail of the scarlet-armoured knight, but unwilling to take the horse by violence, Perceval became so dismayed that he collapsed on the ground and begged the valet to kill him. The valet refused and left Perceval there.

Soon after, a knight passed by on the horse Perceval had wanted, and the valet returned. He said that the knight had stolen the horse from him, and offered to loan Perceval his own poor mount if he would pursue the knight.

GALAHAD RESCUED PERCEVAL, BUT RODE OFF WITHOUT SPEAKING OR REVEALING HIS IDENTITY.

BELOW: Parsifal (Perceval) is depicted here as a great hero, but he seems to have spent much of the Grail Quest throwing tantrums.

Perceval agreed, but when he caught up the knight charged at him – again killing his mount. The knight rode off into the forest, and Perceval lost his trail, leading to another fit of despair.

Perceval is Tempted by the Devil

While he was in the forest, Perceval met what he thought was a woman but was in fact the Devil, who offered him a horse if he would swear to do her bidding if she summoned him. Perceval swore his pledge and was given a fine black horse. Coming to a fast-flowing stream, he crossed himself as his mount prepared to plunge in. This drove the Devil out of him and into the water, which burned for a time. The Devil's plan had been to send him to his death in the river and take his soul. Perceval spent the night in prayer to give thanks for his deliverance, and in the morning revealed that he had somehow come to be atop a mountain surrounded by sea.

BELOW: Perceval was repeatedly tricked and tempted by the Devil, who often took female form when doing so. His habit of crossing himself saved his life on more than one occasion.

The mountain was inhabited by all manner of fearsome creatures, including winged serpents, and Perceval realized that he would not be able to defend himself against them. So he decided to trust in divine protection, and also to climb to the highest point he could find. As he did so, he witnessed a lion and a winged serpent fighting one another and decided – as Yvain had in the same circumstances – to assist the lion, as it was a more natural and trustworthy creature.

This lion, like Yvain's, seemed grateful for the rescue and followed Perceval for a time before returning to its lair. He spent the day in prayer until the lion came back and kept him company as he slept. During the night, he had a dream in which a woman riding a lion told him he would soon fight a terrible foe, and one riding a serpent demanded an explanation from him of why he had slain her flying serpent. Perceval's reason was that the lion was the nobler of the beasts he saw fighting and less likely to do him harm. The lady wanted him to become her servant in recompense; Perceval refused.

The next day, a white ship approached and Perceval asked its master for passage off the island. The master, who was clad in white like a priest, explained that Perceval had been put on the island as a test and would be released just as soon as God wished it. He did offer to advise Perceval on whatever subject might be

ABOVE: **The Grail Quest is liberally strewn with lectures from priests and holy men, who explain to the heroes (and the reader) what they are doing wrong. Perceval was eventually delivered from the island by one such character.**

necessary. After talking for a long time, Perceval asked him the meaning of his dream.

The wise man explained that the lion-riding woman represented Christianity, and came to warn Perceval in straightforward terms that he would soon do battle with the Devil himself. The serpent-riding woman represented the Devil, and in particular the sins of badly misunderstood or corrupted religion. The ship and its master went away, and soon after another ship – this one black – approached.

Aboard this ship was a woman who said she would tell Perceval about the knight he sought if he would swear to do the knight's bidding after she summoned him. He agreed, and she told him that the knight had defeated two others but lost his horse in a river. She then pointed out that Perceval needed to get off the island and offered to help him. Perceval declined, saying that he would stay there until God delivered him from it.

The woman told Perceval that she had once been a servant in the house of a very rich man, who had driven her into the wilderness for displeasing him. Since then she had made war upon him, gathering knights and soldiers to help her cause. She reminded Perceval that all the Knights of the Round Table took an oath to help women who needed it, and he agreed that he was bound to assist her. She then gave him food and wine, and began to seduce him. Seeing the cross on the pommel of his sword, he crossed himself and instantly was surrounded by foul-smelling smoke. Perceval called out to Christ to help him, and saw the woman's illusions melting away.

The ship sailed away, leaving only angry words from the woman aboard it. Dismayed that he was still stuck on the island Perceval tried to kill himself, slashing his leg with his sword. He spent the rest of the day lamenting his sins, and at nightfall bound up his wound to slow the bleeding. The night was spent in prayer, and the next day the white ship came back. Its master explained that the woman on the black ship was the Devil, trying to lead him into temptation. He then delivered a lengthy lecture about the nature of the Devil and how he tried to recruit worthy

OPPOSITE: Perceval's sister led him, along with Bors and Galahad, to a wondrous ship wherein a magical sword awaited. The vessel would kill any man of insufficient piety who entered it.

PERCEVAL DECLARED HE WOULD STAY ON THE ISLAND UNTIL GOD DELIVERED HIM FROM IT.

men to fight against God. Finally the wise man disappeared and the ship conveyed Perceval from the island.

Lancelot Tries to Repent

Lancelot, in the meantime, had also been told by a holy man that his chivalry (meaning his skill at arms) was no use on this quest unless it was accompanied by piety and goodness. He was furnished with arms and sent on his way, and soon afterwards met a valet who reprimanded him at length for his failure to respond to the sight of the Holy Grail. Lancelot prayed for redemption from his state of wickedness, and presently came upon a hermitage with a chapel.

A holy man there recognized Lancelot's sinful state and had much to say about it, but was sad because the hermit whose abode this was had died wearing a fine linen shirt, thus breaking the vows of his holy order. This was clearly the work of the Devil, so the holy man conjured him up and demanded an explanation.

The hermit, explained the Devil, had been a high nobleman before taking holy vows, and had briefly returned to arms to help his nephew defeat his enemies. They found out who he was and attempted to take revenge upon him. However, by a miracle, his robe became impervious to their sword blows. His enemies took away his shirt of sackcloth and tried to burn him alive wearing the shirt of linen that they forced upon him. He died, but his body and the shirt remained untouched.

The Devil then departed, and Lancelot helped bury the hermit's body. The holy man told him that he had already failed in the Grail Quest as he was too sinful and would not be able to see the holy vessel. The holy man also delivered a lecture about virtues such as patience, charity and humility, which Lancelot had once possessed, but had wasted. He said that the instrument of Lancelot's corruption was Guinevere, who had not gone to confession since she was married. He also suggested that Lancelot

BELOW: Lancelot was one of the greatest warriors of his age, but was repeatedly informed by holy men that his skill at arms was worth nothing unless accompanied by a pious and godly soul. He was unable to achieve anything until he had repented.

wear the hermit's hair shirt as a sign of his sincerity in seeking absolution for his sins.

Travelling onwards, Lancelot encountered the formerly sick knight who had taken his sword. The knight immediately attacked him. Lancelot knocked him off his mount, and rode on after tying the knight's horse to a tree so that he could find it when he recovered from the blow Lancelot had given him. He then came to yet another hermitage where he told the story of his adventures thus far to a hermit.

GALAHAD WAS REWARDED BY GOD FOR HIS PIETY. LANCELOT THE SINNER WAS NOT FAVOURED.

Lancelot made a full confession, and told the hermit of a curious dream he had the previous night that featured two knights and seven kings. The hermit then recounted the tale of the seven kings, who were Lancelot's ancestors going all the way back to Joseph of Arimathea. The older of the two knights was Lancelot himself; the younger was Lancelot's son

LEFT: Lancelot came upon a mysterious tournament and naturally joined in. Although he fought well enough to impress all the onlookers, he could inflict no harm on his opponents due to his lack of faith.

Galahad. Galahad in the dream was rewarded by God for his piety, while Lancelot was not favoured by the Almighty.

Travelling onwards, Lancelot came across a huge tournament in which two teams of knights – one side in black and the other in white – were battling one another in a joust. Seeing that one side was losing, Lancelot decided to help them out and charged into the fray. Although he fought so well that onlookers said he had won the honour of the tournament, he did not seem to be able to hurt his opponents no matter how fiercely he struck them.

LANCELOT WAS CONFIDENT THAT GOD WOULD SHOW HIM THE WAY FORWARDS.

In time Lancelot became exhausted and was taken prisoner, which had never happened to him in a tournament before. He blamed this on his sins, but then had a dream in which a holy man berated him for his lack of faith. Pressing on, he met a holy woman and asked her about the incident. She explained that the tournament had a religious significance. The knights in black (whom Lancelot had assisted) were those who had many sins, while those in white were pure. The tournament was also a metaphor for Lancelot's own path, veering between sin and righteousness.

Warned of the dangers of turning away from the path of righteousness, Lancelot reached the River Marcoise. As he pondered how to cross, a knight in black armour rode up and killed his horse, then sped away. Lancelot decided that this was God's will and was not unduly dismayed. He was confident that God would show him the path onwards in due course.

Gawain and Hector Find No Adventures

Gawain, in the meantime, had no adventures of note for many days, which seemed strange to him. Meeting Hector de Mares, he discovered that the same was happening to other knights. Riding together for a week they still found no adventure until they spent the night in a ruined chapel. There, both had visions. Gawain's vision was of a huge herd of bulls, of which all but three were spotted. The bulls were eating at a trough, but spread out to find better food; many of them did not return, and those that did were starving.

LEFT: The tale of Gawain and the Green Knight is a side-story in which Gawain is tricked into a contest with a green knight, who can survive having his head chopped off, whilst Gawain cannot.

Hector's vision was of himself and Lancelot leaving their high seats and riding out, searching for something they could not find. Lancelot suffered many misfortunes and fell from his horse, while Hector tried to attend a wedding feast at a rich man's house. He was told that one of his high station could not enter and was turned away. Hoping to find a holy man to explain these visions, the two rode on, instead coming upon a knight who demanded they joust with him. Gawain did so, and ran him through with his lance, although Gawain himself was unhorsed.

The dying knight asked to be taken to a nearby abbey, which suited Gawain and Hector. There, the knight asked who he had fought, and revealed himself to be Yvain, son of King Urien.

Gawain told Yvain who he was, and Yvain said he was pleased to have met his end at the hands of such a worthy knight. Despite being members of the Round Table, they had failed to recognize one another even after removing their helms.

Saddened, Gawain and Hector found a hermit to ask about their visions and were told that the bulls represented the Knights of the Round Table, who had become proud rather than humble as they should be. The spotted bulls were knights befouled by sin;

RIGHT: **Kings Ban and Bors were allies of Arthur. Ban was the father of Lancelot and (by another woman) also of Hector. King Bors was his brother, and the father of the Round Table knight Bors.**

the three white ones (of which one was only a little spotted and the other two pure white) were the knights who could complete the Grail Quest. Perceval and Galahad were the white bulls; they had no sin. Bors was the slightly spotted one; he had sinned in the past but made amends. The hermit explained that the sinful knights sought the Grail for worldly reasons, such as glory or reward, but only those who sought it out of pure and heavenly motives could find it.

LANCELOT HAD REPENTED OF HIS SINFUL PRIDE, BUT HECTOR HAD NOT.

Hector's vision showed that he and Lancelot had left behind their high station at the Round Table, riding out on steeds of pride and arrogance; Lancelot's fall from his horse indicated that he had repented of his sinful pride, but Hector had not and would thus fail to achieve anything useful on the quest. Gawain and Hector resolved to go back to Camelot, since they could not complete the quest.

Bors Wins the Approval of a Holy Man

Bors de Gaunes met a holy man who was riding on an ass, and told him of the quest. This holy man informed Bors that anyone attempting the Grail Quest in a state of mortal sin was a fool and would achieve worse than nothing. These sinful knights would fall into greater sin as a result of posing as righteous heroes, and would win nothing but dishonour. He also delivered a lecture on how confession cast out the Devil and let Jesus Christ take his place.

The holy man approved of Bors undertaking the quest, for he was of good family and a righteous man. He gave Bors bread and water, saying that a pious knight should not eat rich food, as it could lead to luxury and sin. Bors undertook to eat only bread and water until the quest was over, and confessed his few sins. Although marginally less chaste than Perceval and Galahad, he was close enough to be able to continue with his quest.

Riding on, Bors witnessed a strange event in which a bird returned to its nest to find its young dead. It pecked itself until it bled to death, and the young birds were revived by its blood. Soon afterwards, he stayed at the house of a lady whose sister was making war upon her. The lady needed a knight to fight for her against Priadan le Noir, her sister's champion.

The sister had been the wife of King Amanz, and had introduced unjust and evil customs to the land, resulting in her banishment. The lady had then administered the lands of the king until his death, but now her sister had returned and was taking all she had previously owned back by force. Bors naturally said he would help her.

It is notable that in this case the righteousness of the cause is highlighted – the sister wanted to return the land to evil, so Bors was not merely fighting to prevent an injustice or because a lady had asked him to. Before going to bed that night, Bors prayed for divine assistance in the coming challenge, where in other tales knights were wont to simply get stuck in. He was rewarded with visions in his sleep, offering somewhat cryptic advice on how to act in a future dilemma.

After a formal challenge, Bors and Priadan fought one another. After both were unhorsed, they battled on foot with swords. Seeing that Priadan was skilled in the defence, Bors let him tire himself out by receiving many blows, then counterattacked when Priadan weakened. Once his enemy had surrendered, Bors forced the lords and vassals of the land to swear their allegiance to the lady he had assisted, and thus pacified the people.

Moving on, Bors encountered two knights who had captured his brother Lyonel. Before he could go to help him he also saw a woman being carried off by a knight. She called to him for assistance, creating a dilemma for Bors. Asking that Jesus protect his brother while he rescued the maiden, Bors fought the knight and easily defeated him. The maiden asked that he take her home, and soon afterwards they met some knights who were searching for her.

Bors then went searching for his brother and met a holy man who showed him where to find Lyonel's body. They took him to a chapel and the holy man explained Bors' visions. He would, he

BELOW: **The lady of the castle and all her handmaidens threatened to hurl themselves from the battlements if Bors would not love her. This turned out to be another devilish trick to corrupt a Grail hero.**

LEFT: Bors and Lyonel were about to fight to the death when a thunderbolt from heaven separated them and set their shields afire. Lyonel apparently escaped retribution after killing a Round Table knight and a holy man.

was told, reject a lady who loved him so as to gain a reputation for chastity, and this would bring disaster to many and death to Lancelot.

Given hospitality in a nearby tower, Bors was introduced to the lady he had been told about. She asked him to give her his love, and he declined since his brother lay dead in the chapel. She insisted that he must, since she loved him greatly, and, when he again refused, she and her damsels threatened to hurl themselves off the battlements. Still Bors refused, and they jumped to their deaths. Crossing himself, Bors felt the enchantment he had been under break; this episode had all been a trick of the Devil intended to draw him away from the righteous path.

LYONEL'S CAPTORS WERE STRUCK MIRACULOUSLY DEAD AND HE WAS RESTORED TO LIBERTY.

Bors' brother was no longer in the chapel, causing him to wonder if Lyonel really was dead. He pressed on and came to an abbey whose friars explained the visions and strange happenings.

The self-sacrificial bird was a metaphor for Christ, of course, saving the human race by choosing to die. Bors' battle against Priadan represented him fighting to defend the church from the sins of humans. Lyonel was alive, the abbot told Bors, but he was without Christian virtue, so Bors was correct in choosing to save the damsel instead. In doing so, he had done God's work and was rewarded; Lyonel's captors were struck miraculously dead and he was once more at liberty.

Next, Bors arrived at a castle where a tournament was to be held and he found his brother at the chapel. Lyonel was angry that Bors had left him in captivity, and would not listen to any explanation. He armed himself and prepared to fight, but Bors would not. Lyonel rode him down, and Bors was trampled by his horse. A holy man tried to save Bors, so Lyonel killed him and would have beheaded Bors if not for the intervention of Calogrenant.

Calogrenant was a Knight of the Round Table and a friend of Bors. Lyonel attacked him and after a long fight slew him. Bors was weak as a result of being trampled, and more inclined to pray than to fight. He begged God's mercy for fighting his brother and prepared to defend himself, but the two were separated by a lightning bolt from heaven that burned their shields. A heavenly voice commanded Bors to go and find Perceval, so he left Lyonel to take care of the bodies and went to the seashore, where he found a boat waiting. Bors fell asleep in the boat, and when he woke Perceval was there, although neither was sure how the other had come aboard.

BELOW: A depiction of the knighting of Sir Galahad. Traditionally a knight received his sword and spurs – essentially his badges of office – at the time he was knighted. The sword and the horse have always been associated with nobility.

Galahad Finds Bors and Perceval

Galahad, in the meantime, had apparently found numerous adventures, although the author declines to tell us about them as it would take too long. At length, he came to a castle whose garrison were under heavy attack, and decided to help them. Gawain and Hector, presumably on their way back to Camelot, had also chanced upon the battle but had decided to join the attackers. Not recognizing them, Galahad attacked Gawain and rendered him unconscious, killing his horse in the same stroke.

Gawain recovered consciousness and realized that he had taken a blow from the sword that Galahad had pulled from the stone, just as predicted. The knights of the castle took Gawain inside and cared for him, even though he had fought against them. Hector remained there, too, until Gawain was healed.

Galahad chased the attackers when they fled, and afterwards rode aimlessly for a time before meeting a damsel who led him to the shore. There, he found a ship; Perceval and Bors were already

BELOW: Preparations for the beginning of the Grail Quest were an occasion for pageantry, with grand oaths sworn on holy relics and, no doubt, proud boasts of impending success. Many of the knights did not return to Camelot, meeting misadventure on the road somewhere.

aboard. The vessel sailed fast for some time and came to an island where another ship lay. The damsel told the three knights that an adventure awaited them aboard it, and eventually revealed that she was Perceval's sister and the daughter of King Pellehen. She told the knights that they must be free of sin and steadfast in their belief if they entered this ship, or they would die.

Inside the ship was a couch upon which lay a crown and a sword, whose grip was fashioned from the bones of strange creatures. These had the properties of making the bearer immune to heat, and also causing him to forget everything except the purpose for which he gripped the weapon.

THE SWORD HAD DELIVERED ONLY ONE STROKE IN LOGRES, TURNING THE LAND AROUND INTO A WASTELAND.

Inscriptions on the sword said that no-one could grasp it unless his skill surpassed all others, and that anyone who drew the sword would soon die unless he was better at fighting than everyone else. Perceval and Bors tried to take the sword and could not. Galahad declined to try.

Perceval's sister told the knights that the sword had only delivered one stroke in Logres. This was carried out by King Varlan, a former Saracen who had converted to Christianity. He was warring with King Lambar, father of the Fisher King. All but defeated, Varlan had seized this sword from the ship and attacked Lambar, cutting right through him and his horse – and on into the ground – with a single blow. The realms of both kings were devastated by this blow, becoming a pestilential wasteland. Varlan collapsed dead soon after returning the sword to the ship.

There were other dire warnings on the sword and its belt, telling of how the weapon would fail he who prized it the most, and would be a curse upon him to whom the sword should be the greatest blessing. An inscription also stated that the belt it was carried upon could only be removed by a virgin daughter of royalty, and that her fate would be terrible if she ceased to be chaste.

Percival's sister explained that there was no danger in taking the sword, as the events mentioned in the inscriptions had already happened long ago. The first disaster happened to Nascien, brother-in-law to King Mordrain, when he was fighting a giant. He prized the sword most highly, since it offered him a means to win an apparently hopeless battle, and thus it broke and failed him. The second incident involved Parlan, now known as the Fisher King. He had found the sword and started to draw it when he was struck in the thighs by a supernatural lance. This was how he became the Fisher King, or the Crippled King, and thus the sword was a curse to him.

At this point in the tale the author describes how the couch included posts of wood that were of different colours, and goes off on a tangent as he explains how this came to be. This lengthy tale starts in the Garden of Eden and explains how the ship was built.

It is, however, not particularly relevant to the Grail Quest. The knights learned of these things by way of a letter found under the crown on the couch before Perceval's sister girded upon Galahad the sword they had found, and the ship landed in Scotland.

In Scotland, Galahad and his companions immediately fell afoul of a town full of hostile knights. Defeating the first 10 that attacked them, the Grail knights took their horses and advanced into the castle where they fought and defeated the garrison. The Grail knights felt remorse for the vast number of enemies they had slain, but reasoned that it was God's will that this had happened. A holy man at the castle then explained that the town had been ruled by three brothers who hated God, which

ABOVE: **The Grail Ship conveyed Galahad and his companions to Scotland, where they dealt with some wicked enemies of God before proceeding on towards the castle of the Grail King.**

made Galahad feel much better about killing them. The brothers
had committed a veritable catalogue of sins, including incest
with their sister, wounding their father, destroying chapels and
attacking abbots.

The former lord of the town, who was dying, told Galahad
that heaven rejoiced that the wicked brothers and their knights
had been slain, and that now the three Grail knights should go to
the castle of the Fisher King. They entered the Forest Gaste and
were shown the way by the White Stag, who was escorted by four
lions. Led to a chapel, they took part in a Mass at which all three
had visions that were later interpreted as yet another metaphor
for Christianity.

Leaving the chapel, the grail knights
came to a castle whose lord insisted that
every passing virgin fill a basin with
blood from her arm. The 10 knights
from the castle who blocked the road
said that Perceval's sister would have to
do so, and the Grail knights declined. A fight broke out, with the
10 getting much the worst of it, but they were reinforced by 60 of
their fellows coming from the castle.

> THE KNIGHTS PLACED THE
> BODY OF PERCEVAL'S SISTER
> IN A BOAT AS SHE HAD
> REQUESTED.

The battle raged until nightfall, at which time the lord of
the castle invited Galahad and his companions to enjoy his
hospitality under a truce. Over dinner he explained that a lady
of the castle was gravely ill, and could only be cured by the blood
of a maiden who was a virgin in body and spirit, the daughter of
royalty and Perceval's sister.

Perceval's sister decided to comply with the request, and
gave her blood the next day. She fainted for lack of blood and
realized she was dying. Giving instructions for how to treat her
body, she urged the Grail knights to press on with their quest.
The knights placed the body of Perceval's sister in a boat and set
it adrift as she had requested. They did not return to the castle,
but sheltered in a chapel nearby as a storm blew up. When it was
over, the castle was destroyed and everyone in it was dead.

The knights found the graves of the many virgins who had
died the same way, failing to heal the lady of the castle. They
concluded that the destruction was Godly vengeance, for

OPPOSITE: **The Grail
Quest presents Galahad
as an unstoppable
righteous force capable
of overcoming any
obstacle. Here, he is
depicted battling 40
knights simultaneously;
even the greatest of the
Round Table knights are
no match for him.**

Perceval's sister had died giving blood to heal a lady who was a terrible sinner. The knights decided to press on separately. Bors went to help a wounded knight who was fleeing another, and soon afterwards Galahad and Perceval separated.

Lancelot's Voyage

Lancelot remained by the River Marcoise for a time, until a heavenly voice told him to go to the river and board a boat he found there. He did so, and fell asleep. When he awoke, he found that there was a maiden in the boat. She was dead, and a paper close by her said that she was Perceval's sister. Lancelot read of the adventures his friends had so far shared, and soon encountered a holy man who warned him of the dangers of falling back into his former sinful ways.

Lancelot spent a month in the boat, praying and receiving divine favour, before he spotted a knight approaching on the river bank. The knight, who turned out to be Galahad, entered the boat, and the two of them sailed in it for half a year. The author tells us that they had many adventures in which they prevailed mainly through divine favour, but declines to tell us any more about them. Eventually Galahad left to continue his quest, and Lancelot sailed on alone, but for the body of Perceval's sister.

Lancelot eventually came to a town, where he found the gate guarded by two lions. Drawing his sword, he planned to fight them,

but was chided by a heavenly voice for being such a fool as to trust his sword over God's mercy. He sheathed the weapon and swore not to draw it again. The lions did not harm him, but he found the town empty.

Searching the palace, Lancelot came to a chamber in which Mass was being held with angels present. Although warned by a voice not to enter, Lancelot did so in order to help the priest, who was in difficulty. He was flung out of the chamber and found the next morning by the townspeople, alive but unable to move

or speak. He stayed that way for 24 days before recovering, one
day for each year he had served the Devil by being filled with sin.

Lancelot discovered that he was at the town of King Pelles,
father of Perceval. The Grail was there, too, and it filled the
tables with bounty at each meal. One evening, a knight came
to the doors of the castle, but they closed themselves against
him. The king told him to go away, for he was too full of sin to
enter while the Grail was present. The knight was Hector, whose
dream had predicted these events. Afterwards, Lancelot returned
to Camelot and told of his adventures.

Galahad Performs Wonders

Galahad, after leaving Lancelot in the boat, came to the abbey
where King Mordrain waited. After speaking with Galahad,
for whom he had waited so many years, Mordrain finally died.
Galahad then visited a boiling spring that could not harm him;
it cooled and was known by his name afterward. At an abbey
he rescued his ancestor Simeon, who had been condemned to
burn for hundreds of years for having sinned against Joseph of
Arimathea.

Galahad then joined Perceval, and for five years they
travelled the land having various adventures and putting right

numerous wrongs, so that Logres was thereafter more peaceful and adventures were rarer. Finally, they met Bors and went to Corbenic, castle of the Fisher King.

There, Galahad and his companions sat down to dinner with King Pelles. All those who were not holy and righteous were told

to leave the hall as the Grail would soon be among them. The few remaining were joined by nine knights who had come to enjoy the feast. Three were from Denmark, three from Gaul and three from Ireland.

The wounded Fisher King was brought out of his bed and greeted Galahad, for whom he had long waited. All those who were not companions of the Grail Quest left the hall. Among them appeared Josephe, the first Christian bishop, attended by angels.

The angels brought the Grail and the bleeding lance, and Josephe performed Mass, before disappearing.

The companions then saw Jesus himself, who gave them the sacrament and told them that although some worthy men had in the past partaken of the Grail feast, none had ever sat in the honoured places that Galahad and his companions now occupied. There were 12 knights at this feast, as there had been 12 Apostles at the Last Supper. Jesus told them that they would leave this place to spread the word as the Apostles had done, and all but one of them would die in this service.

Jesus also instructed Galahad to heal the Fisher King with blood from the lance, which he did. The king then left the castle to join a community of White Friars where many miracles were performed. The 12 knights who had been at the feast dispersed, and Galahad, Bors and Perceval returned to the ship where they had found the sword. The Grail was there, and while they were aboard the ship set sail.

At length, the companions came to the city of Sarraz, where the first Christian bishop was consecrated. They took the Grail to the temple there, and saw the boat in which they had set Perceval's sister adrift approaching. After burying her, the three were treacherously imprisoned by the king of the city, but were sustained in luxury by the Grail. Nearing death, the king asked for their pardon and died once it was granted.

Galahad was made king of the city and ruled for a

BELOW: A fifteenth century depiction of Galahad and his companions kneeling before the Holy Grail. The story does not go into detail about what became of the other nine knights at the Grail feast.

THE QUEST AS RELIGIOUS METAPHOR

The story of the Grail Quest has a quite different character to the earlier tales. It is less concerned with knightly deeds and more with its underlying religious message – which is pounded home in a heavy-handed manner at every opportunity. The Grail heroes ride from abbey to hermitage, constantly being berated for their sinful ways, or enjoined to behave properly in the future.

The fictional history of 1136 had morphed into a backdrop for knightly adventure tales by 1180, but the Grail Quest of 1210 represents a hijacking of the Arthurian mythos to present a sort of epic parable. There is still violence and adventure, but it is largely glossed over to leave more room for lengthy expositions of religious matters or the heavenly significance of the heroes' actions.

Where the knights of the 1100s tales fight for justice, chivalry and the honour of their lord, those of 1210 seem more concerned with doing the work of the Lord. It is made very clear that nobody can achieve anything while in a state of mortal sin, and there is no shortage of holy men – notably White Friars – ready to remind the knights of this. The writer, it would appear, had an agenda.

ABOVE: **The Grail Quest takes the form of an enormous parable, the lurid violence of earlier tales replaced with rather tedious exposition by holy men and hermits. Its message is clear: nothing of any significance can be achieved by sinners.**

year. Having finally been granted sight of the wonders revealed by the Grail, he prayed to be allowed to die in this finest moment of his life, and after receiving sacrament he parted from his companions for the last time. Even as he fell dead, the Grail and the lance were taken away by a heavenly hand. Perceval lived for three more years as a hermit, and then also died. Bors buried him beside his sister and returned to Camelot where he related his adventures. The Holy Grail was not seen again on Earth.

Quraige Brult noble cheualereux

5

LE MORTE D'ARTHUR

The tale of King Arthur took on what might be considered to be its classic form when an individual known as Sir Thomas Malory wrote *Le Morte d'Arthur*.

The exact identity of Malory is open to question, although he is most commonly identified as a knight who fought in the Wars of the Roses and died in 1471. He seems to have spent a fair amount of time imprisoned, which would give him time to write his epic story. It was published in 1485, with reprints and revised versions following.

Malory drew on the work of Geoffrey of Monmouth and Chrétien de Troyes, of course, but he was also influenced by material added to the Arthurian cycle by others. Notable among these was Robert de Boron, who wrote poems about Merlin and Joseph of Arimathea that became incorporated into the Arthurian mythos. Robert de Boron also added the story of the sword in the stone to the Arthur legend.

OPPOSITE: **Sir Lancelot in action during a tourney, whilst Arthur and Guinevere look on. The later tales relegate Arthur to this sort of passive role – it is his knights that do all the great deeds, whilst he presides over their fellowship.**

WHO WAS THOMAS MALORY?

Other identities have been suggested for Malory, but if he was a knight during the Wars of the Roses (1455–1485) then he would have experience of knighthood at a court riven by internal politics, where friend and foe alike were bound by formal courtesies and where reputation was worth fighting over. He was a knight of much more complex times than Arthur's Saxon-battling followers, and his perspective would be coloured by his own experiences. What is known of Mallory is recorded in The Winchester Manuscript, discovered in 1934 in Winchester College library, in which he is described as a 'knight prisoner'. As well as being a knight, he also owned land and served as a Member of Parliament from 1449. In 1451, he was accused of extortion, burglary and rape, and eventually sentenced to prison for a year. There followed a series of further arrests for various crimes and prison escapes, but he was eventually pardoned by Edward IV in 1461.

BELOW: A statue of the German epic poet Wolfram von Eschenbach. Along with his contemporaries Hartmann von Aue and Gottfried von Strassburg, he contributed significantly to the Arthurian mythos.

The German epic poets Wolfram von Eschenbach, Hartmann von Aue and Gottfried von Strassburg, writing around the year 1200, produced works that drew on earlier Arthurian stories and incorporated traditional tales that were previously unrelated into the Arthurian mythos.

Influences and Borrowed Stories

Other tales became part of the Arthurian mythos by way of both influence and direct incorporation. The Celtic legend of Tristan and Iseult, which tells of a tragic love affair at the court of King Mark of Cornwall, was almost certainly an influence on the romance between Guinevere and Lancelot at Arthur's court. Both tales feature attempts to expose the lovers and a rift between friends caused by the affair. In addition to influencing the Arthur story, the tale of Tristan and Iseult was later incorporated wholesale, with Tristan recast as a Knight of the Round Table.

In the early thirteenth century, several works were produced by multiple authors whose identities remain unclear. These make up what is now often known as the Lancelot-Grail Cycle, or the

Vulgate Cycle. This was in turn reworked later in the century to create the Post-Vulgate cycle, which omits some sections entirely and amends or adds others. The Post-Vulgate Cycle was one of the primary influences on Malory's work.

Alternative versions of some Arthur stories appear, along with many other tales, in the body of Welsh traditional literature known as the *Mabinogion*. This first appeared in written form in the 1300s, but the tales within are much older and draw on ancient Celtic myths in many cases. Even where there is no direct connection between the *Mabinogion* and the Arthurian cycle, parallels can be drawn between many events and characters in both.

Malory thus had many influences and many sources – which were often contradictory – to work with when he wrote *Le Morte d'Arthur*. His version of the story has become the classic one, followed by many later retellings or referred to as a romanticized tale to which a more 'realistic' version is compared. Malory's tale was the first book to be published by William Caxton, who set up the first printing press in England and also became the first seller of printed books. This alone would give *Le Morte d'Arthur* a place in the history books, even if it were not one of the most influential stories of all time.

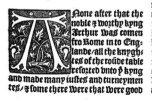

Malory's Arthur story generally follows the outline of Geoffrey of Monmouth's work, beginning with the deeds of Uther Pendragon and ending with the death of Arthur in battle against Mordred. However, Malory introduces many new characters and tells their stories along the way. Not all of these tales are particularly relevant to the overall plotline of Arthur's life; they are tales in their own right set against the backdrop of Arthur's reign. As first published by Caxton, Malory's tale was presented as 21 books, but it was written as eight.

ABOVE: *Le Morte d'Arthur* was the first book published by William Caxton, who introduced the printing press to England. It was enormously important as a historical event regardless of the content of the book.

Arthur Gains His Kingdom

Malory's tale begins with events familiar from Geoffrey of Monmouth's pseudo-history. Uther Pendragon, assisted by Merlin's magic, slept with Igraine (the wife of Gorlois) and conceived Arthur at Tintagel Castle. The boy was fostered to Sir Ector (called Antor in some versions) and became squire to Ector's son Kay when he was old enough. Ector did not know who Arthur's father was; nor did Arthur himself.

In the meantime, Uther grew ill and died, leaving the kingdom in chaos as the great lords vied for power. Merlin solved this problem by magically placing a sword so that it was thrust right through an anvil and into a large stone beneath, inscribing on the blade that it could only be pulled out by the rightful King of England. Various people tried to remove the sword, and of course, all failed.

Arthur grew up ignorant of his lineage but was tutored by Merlin until he reached the age of 15. Still a squire, he went to Westminster (where the sword was) to attend a tournament with Sir Kay. According to some versions of the tale, Kay broke his sword in the fighting; in others he simply forgot to bring it. Either way, Arthur was sent urgently to find a suitable weapon. He pulled the sword out of the anvil without realizing the significance of what he was doing, and brought it to Kay.

THE SWORD IN THE STONE WAS NOT EXCALIBUR, THOUGH SOME VERSIONS OF THE STORY CLAIM OTHERWISE.

Ector knew about the sword and had Arthur put it back then draw it out again. Nobody else could do so, and after repeating the feat in front of lords, knights and clergymen, he was proclaimed King of England. Kay was to be his seneschal. It is notable that this sword was not Excalibur, although some versions of the story assume that it is.

While those who had witnessed Arthur's feat accepted him as king, many of the more distant kings and great lords did not recognize his claim to the throne. They came to Carlion in Wales where Arthur was holding a feast to mark Pentecost and challenged his right to rule. Arthur and his supporters were besieged for a time, before Merlin arrived and predicted victory.

LEFT: Arthur's pulling of the sword from the stone established his right to rule as Uther Pendragon's heir. There were many who did not accept this, however, leading to a period of bloody conflict.

Several hundred knights changed sides to join Arthur, enabling him to defeat his enemies. On Merlin's advice, he let them retreat once they were beaten.

With assistance from Kings Ban and Bors, Arthur confronted his enemies again and fought more bloody battles against them. The armies of 11 kings fought against Arthur, but had to return to their own lands, which had been attacked in their absence. Arthur then marched to the assistance of King Leodegrance, and fell in love with his daughter Guinevere. They were married, and among the gifts given to Arthur by Leodegrance was the Round Table, with seats for 150 knights.

Among the kings who opposed Arthur was King Lot, who was married to Arthur's half-sister Morgause. Arthur did not know they were related and slept with her when she visited his castle. Their child was named Mordred and would ultimately cause Arthur's death. A little later Arthur was introduced to his half-sister Morgan le Fay, who was the daughter of Igraine and Gorlois.

Arthur also encountered King Pellinore, who was engaged in a fruitless mission to hunt the Questing Beast. They met again a little later, this time in combat, and Pellinore won after Arthur's sword broke. Merlin intervened and put Pellinore into a magical sleep, then guided Arthur to the Lady of the Lake, who gave him the magical sword Excalibur. Although the sword was indeed excellent, its scabbard was even better – whoever wore it on his belt could not be wounded.

ABOVE: Arthur was given Excalibur by the Lady of the Lake when his own sword – presumably the one drawn from the stone – broke in a duel with King Pellinore. This was one of the few occasions where Merlin directly aided Arthur.

King Rience, whom Arthur had fought against when he helped Leodegrance, was in the habit of collecting the beards of his enemies and wearing them as a cloak. He sent a demand to Arthur for his beard, threatening to collect it along with Arthur's head if he refused. Arthur naturally did so, leading to war. In the interim, he issued an edict that all noble children born on the day Mordred was due were to be put to death. The babies were rounded up and set adrift in a ship, which was wrecked with Mordred as the only survivor.

The Wounding of the Fisher King

While preparations were being made to fight King Rience, a messenger from the Lady of the Lake arrived bearing another magical sword. This one could only be drawn by the most powerful knight in the world. Sir Balin le Savage, recently released from imprisonment, managed to draw the sword and decided to keep it despite a warning that he would regret the decision.

The Lady of the Lake was in feud with Sir Balin, and came to Camelot requesting his head as repayment for the gift of Excalibur. Balin killed the Lady of the Lake and was banished from court for this crime. Attempting to regain Arthur's favour he captured King Rience after various adventures, but this did not stop the war against his kingdom. King Lot and the other 11 kings who opposed Arthur joined this conflict, but were ultimately defeated. Lot was killed by King Pellinore.

Balin's misfortune continued when an invisible knight killed a man who was under his protection. Seeking vengeance, he followed the knight to the court of Listenoise, home of the Holy Grail, and killed him there. The Grail King broke Balin's sword as punishment, so Balin grabbed the nearest weapon and attacked him. This was the bleeding lance, and with it Balin inflicted the Dolorous Stroke that maimed the Grail King and turned his realm into a wasteland.

BELOW: Sir Balin was a tragic figure cursed by a magic sword. After inflicting the Dolorous Stroke that maimed the Fisher King, he fought against and killed his brother Balan, whom he failed to recognize. The brothers were buried in the same grave.

Afterwards, Balin encountered his brother Balan. They failed to recognize one another and fought. Both received mortal wounds and were buried in the same tomb. The cursed sword that Balin had taken from the damsel was placed in a block of stone by Merlin. It reappeared later in the tale.

The Round Table Established

With his kingdom secured, Arthur began to attract knights to fill the seats around his famous table. Many were the sons of great lords and kings, and some were kings in their own right. Membership of the Round Table was prized more highly by

RIGHT: Nimue learned magic from Merlin then betrayed him and left him entombed. Thereafter she replaced Merlin as magical adviser to Arthur, directly assisting him on several occasions.

some than their own rank. However, in accepting the best knights to be members of the company, Arthur took a grave risk, as many of them were at odds with one another. King Pellinore was a member of the Round Table, but so were Gawain and Gaheris. As the sons of King Lot, killed by Pellinore, they wanted revenge, but were prepared to bide their time.

Pellinore, in the meantime, pursued his hunt of the Questing Beast to the exclusion of almost all else. This caused him to ignore a lady's cries for help, to his great shame. Soon after this incident, Arthur began the practice of all Round Table knights swearing to uphold good conduct and help those in need. These oaths would be renewed each year at Pentecost, and thus became known as the Pentecostal Oath.

ABOVE: Morgan le Fay attempted to steal Excalibur whilst Arthur slept, but since he was holding the grip, she had to be content with just the scabbard. This left Arthur vulnerable to wounds and ultimately permitted Mordred to kill him.

The Lady of the Lake killed by Balin was replaced by another, named Nimue, and Merlin fell in love with her. He knew she would be his undoing, but could not resist her. So he taught her magic, and she used it to imprison him in a cave or under a great rock. After this, she assumed Merlin's role as adviser and protector to Arthur.

After defeating an attempt by five northern kings to depose or kill him, Arthur went hunting with King Uriens and Sir Accolon. They were deceived and captured, although Uriens was magically returned to Camelot to be with his wife, Morgan le Fay. Arthur was imprisoned in a castle whose lord was feuding with his brother. He was a thoroughly bad character, who had resorted to imprisoning knights until they agreed to fight for him. Arthur said he would if all the prisoners were released.

As well as being wife to King Uriens, Morgan le Fay was also lover to Sir Accolon. He was imprisoned elsewhere and agreed to

WAR WITH ROME

As told in Geoffrey of Monmouth's pseudo-history, ambassadors from Rome arrived at Camelot and demanded tribute. Arthur refused and prepared to make war on Rome. In Malory's version there are incidents told of previously by Geoffrey; Arthur's dream of the bear and dragon was repeated, as was the fight with a giant atop Mont St. Michel. However, in Malory's version it was a boar that fought the dragon.

The war also took the same general course as that told of by Geoffrey. An escalating fight was started at the parlay; a battle was fought when the convoy of prisoners was attacked, and Arthur finally defeated Lucius. However, in this version he actually reached Rome and was crowned emperor. Leaving trusted men to run the new territories, Arthur then returned home.

fight not knowing that it was Arthur he was facing. Morgan le Fay knew, and sent him Excalibur whose scabbard would protect him. Arthur had perhaps unwisely given his magical sword to Morgan le Fay for safekeeping. She gave Arthur back a replica she had made and kept the original.

Arthur, thinking he was armed with Excalibur, was wounded when he thought he was invincible, and his false sword then broke on Accolon's helm. He fought on with the stump, and was saved by Nimue, the Lady of the Lake, who caused Accolon to drop Excalibur. Accolon died from his wounds and Arthur swore vengeance against Morgan le Fay.

Thinking Arthur was dead, Morgan le Fay decided to rid herself of her husband, King Uriens. She was prevented by their son Uwaine and sent to a convent for her crime. Instead, she went to where Arthur was recovering from his wounds and stole the scabbard of Excalibur. Although pursued, she escaped after hurling the scabbard into a lake.

Morgan le Fay then sent Arthur a cloak that would kill him if he wore it, but he was again saved by Nimue. He banished Sir Uwaine in case he was in league with his mother, causing Uwaine's cousin Gawain to leave as well. After various adventures they returned to court.

Lancelot, Gareth and Tristan

Three of Malory's eight books are focused on the deeds of individuals. The first to receive this treatment was Lancelot du Lac. The son of King Ban, the infant Lancelot was separated from his parents as they were fleeing enemies and was rescued by the Lady of the Lake. He was thus raised in magical surroundings before going to Camelot to be knighted.

Lancelot fell in love with Guinevere as soon as he arrived, but also became great friends with Arthur. He was desired by Morgan le Fay, who at one point enchanted him to stay asleep while she captured him. He escaped with the help of the daughter of King

Bagdemagus, although he had to agree to fight in a tournament on Bagdemagus' behalf in return.

Lancelot was notable for strictly adhering to the Pentecostal Oath sworn by Arthur's knights. He would always help a lady who asked him, even if the situation was dire, or there was trickery involved. One lady he helped betrayed him to the villainous Sir Phelot by asking Lancelot to retrieve her hawk from a tree. He had to remove his arms and armour to climb the tree, and was then set upon by Phelot. Lancelot won the fight using a tree branch.

In the course of his adventures, Lancelot rescued Sir Kay on more than one occasion, and at one point 'borrowed' his amour while they were in camp. Lancelot wanted to avoid being recognized for who he was and thought the guise of Sir Kay might help. This led to a misunderstanding where other Knights of the Round Table thought he was a villain who had murdered Kay.

During his many adventures he went to the castle of the Grail King, but because of his love for another man's wife (whether or not adultery occurred remains an open question) he could not properly appreciate what he saw. He was tricked by magic into thinking he was sleeping with Guinevere when it was in fact Elaine, daughter of the Grail King. She bore him a son, who was named Galahad.

Soon after, both Lancelot and Elaine attended a feast held by King Arthur to honour his victory in France, and she plotted to bring Lancelot to her bed, even though he had eyes only for Guinevere. This led to an embarrassing incident where Lancelot, talking in his sleep of his love for Guinevere while in bed with Elaine, was overheard by Guinevere in the next room.

BELOW: Arguably, Lancelot is the central figure of the Arthurian legends. He is an invincible warrior who has many of the best adventures, including being magically put to sleep by Morgan le Fay and fathering Galahad whilst enchanted.

ABOVE: Lancelot
preferred to go incognito
or in disguise as much
as possible, since his
reputation could be a
burden. He disguised
himself as Sir Kay on
one occasion, leading to
other knights thinking
Kay had been murdered
and his armour stolen.

OPPOSITE: Lancelot was
tricked into sleeping
with Elaine, daughter
of the Grail King.
He treated her rather
badly, though they
were apparently happy
together for a time at the
castle of Joyous Gard.

Guinevere confronted Lancelot and reprimanded him so vigorously that he went mad and ran off into the forest where he lived as a wild man for the next two years. Knights went to find him, including Perceval, who received grievous wounds jousting with Sir Ector. Both were healed when the Holy Grail appeared to Perceval.

Lancelot came upon Sir Bliant, and in his confused state tried to take his sword and shield. Bliant resisted, but was overcome by the crazed Lancelot. With assistance from other knights, he managed to get Lancelot to a castle where he was chained to a bed to prevent him from running off again. There, he was fed and looked after in his madness, and he repaid his rescuers well. Out of the window Lancelot one day saw Sir Bliant battling six knights. He broke his chains, leaped out of the window and put them to flight, saving Bliant.

Eventually, while running wild, Lancelot was found by Elaine and brought to her father's castle, where he was restored to sanity by the Holy Grail. He asked her forgiveness for the way he had treated her, and together they moved into a castle that had once been named Dolorous Gard, but was now Joyous Gard.

Holding a tournament, Lancelot was reunited with some of his old companions, who told him how vigorously they had sought him. He decided to return to Camelot where he was welcomed. With him he brought his son Galahad to be trained as a knight.

Gareth of Orkney

The story of Gareth of Orkney began when a young man came to court, but would not give his name. Sir Kay was quite cruel to him and nicknamed him Beaumains ('White Hands') but

Lancelot and Gawain liked him. Gareth mostly lived in the kitchens and seemed to favour the company of commoners. This led many to think he was not a nobleman at all.

Eventually a lady came to court asking for assistance against the Red Knight of the Red Lands who was besieging the castle of her sister, Lady Lyonesse. Gareth said he would do it, although his offer was not well received. On the way, Gareth encountered Sir Kay and Sir Lancelot. Kay insulted Gareth, still thinking he was of low station, and Gareth unhorsed him in a joust. He then battled Lancelot to a standstill and they parted company.

Next Gareth met the Black Knight, who challenged him and was killed. His brother, the Green Knight, tried to take revenge and was bested. Gareth ordered him to go to Camelot and swear allegiance to Arthur. Much the same happened when his brothers the Blue and Red Knights attacked.

Finally, Gareth reached Castle Perilous, which was under siege by the Knight of the Red Lands. Gareth challenged him and was victorious, agreeing to spare the Knight of the Red Lands so long as he returned all the territory he had taken from Lady Lyonesse and went to swear allegiance to Arthur at Camelot.

Lady Lyonesse held a tournament, which Gareth wanted to enter incognito. He was assisted in this by a magic ring that changed his appearance, and won honour and glory for himself by defeating many Round Table knights. Gareth was eventually revealed to be the son of King Lot and Morgause, and thus a relative of King Arthur. He and his brother Gawain fought but stopped when they realized one another's identity. Eventually, Gareth married lady Lyonesse and joined the company of the Round Table.

BELOW: Although some suspected he was a commoner, Gareth of Orkney was a ferocious fighter who could give even Lancelot a hard battle. He won his station at the Round Table on his own merit before revealing his heritage.

The Tale of Sir Tristan

Sir Tristan (or Tristram) was a nephew of King Mark of Cornwall, and a master of many skills including playing the harp. He came to prominence when he represented his uncle's kingdom in a joust against Marhaus, champion of the King of Ireland. Tristan defeated Marhaus by stabbing him through the head. Marhaus lived long enough to return home, and his sister, the Queen of Ireland, swore vengeance on Tristan.

Tristan, meanwhile, was suffering from the effects of poison that had been on Marhaus' lance and he went to Ireland to seek a cure. He was tended by the Irish king's daughter Isolde (Iseult or Isoud in other versions of the tale), and they fell in love. The Queen of Ireland discovered who Tristan was when she noted that a piece was missing from the tip of his sword. It fitted with a fragment removed from the skull of Sir Marhaus.

Returning to Cornwall, Tristan found himself at odds with King Mark over a woman. She was the wife of a nobleman, and both wanted to have an affair with her. Neither did, but King Mark began to hate Tristan and eventually sent him to Ireland to bring Isolde to Cornwall. Tristan obeyed, and despite the fact that the King of Ireland wanted Tristan to marry Isolde (he hated Tristan a lot less than his wife did), he agreed that his daughter should wed Mark of Cornwall.

After the marriage of Isolde and Mark, she ran afoul of Sir Palomides, who had courted her in Ireland before Tristan arrived. She was rescued by Tristan and brought back to King Mark. Their adulterous relationship was eventually discovered, causing Mark to attack Tristan. After losing several knights, Mark agreed to make peace. This only lasted for a while; Tristan was caught seeing Isolde and taken to a chapel near the sea. He escaped by jumping from a cliff into the sea, but was injured in the process.

Isolde, in the meantime, was punished by being sent to a leper colony, from which Tristan rescued her. They lived in a forest

ABOVE: **In some versions of the tale, Tristan meets his end when King Mark treacherously stabs him in the back whilst he plays the harp for Isolde. King Mark is a thorough villain in all variants.**

TRISTAN FOUND HIMSELF AT ODDS WITH KING MARK OVER A DAMSEL.

for a time, but eventually King Mark found Isolde while Tristan was away and brought her back to his court. Tristan had been shot with a poisoned arrow and needed help, so he went to the court of King Howell in Brittany. King Howell's daughter, Isolde of the White Hands, healed his wound.

It is notable that Malory did not mind using similar or even near-identical names in his tales. There are numerous ladies named Elaine, for example, and in Gareth's tale there is a Red Knight and a Red Knight of the Red Lands. Here, there are two Isoldes who are quite different people, although both loved Tristan.

ABOVE: The tragic romance of Tristan and Isolde was not originally part of the Arthurian legend, though it strongly influenced the Lancelot-Guinevere story. This created conflicts when the Tristan-Isolde tale was shoehorned in as well.

Ill-Matched Marriage

Tristan married Isolde of the White Hands, but loved her less than he did the other Isolde. He adventured for a time with Sir Lamorak, son of King Pellinore. Their exploits included saving the people of an island from a giant knight. They also encountered Sir Palomides, who was pursuing the Questing Beast. He defeated both with ease and left them to continue his quest.

Tristan was offered the chance to join the Round Table after defeating Sir Kay and Sir Tor in a joust. They spoke ill of Cornish knights, so he challenged and unseated them. Not believing himself worthy, Tristan declined and went to Cornwall where he resumed his affair with Isolde. He was accompanied by his wife's brother, Kahedin, who also fell in love with Isolde. Tristan found one of his letters to her and, in a truly breathtaking piece of hypocrisy, accused the woman with whom he was having an adulterous affair of being unfaithful to him with his wife's brother.

Unable to contain his grief, Tristan went mad and ran off into the forest, where he was tended by the people of a castle. He was eventually brought back to Mark's court and healed of his madness, but was then banished. Tristan went to Camelot where he took part in a tournament. He killed the three sons of Sir Darras in the tourney, and was imprisoned along with Sir Palomides and Sir Dinadan. He became sick and was released on condition that he would protect Sir Darras' remaining sons.

BANISHED FROM KING MARK'S COURT, TRISTAN WENT TO CAMELOT.

Tristan had not been free for long when Morgan le Fay captured him. Her conditions for his release were that he must bear a shield she had made in a coming tournament. The shield bore a device that alluded to Lancelot's adultery with the queen, and King Arthur would see it at the tournament. He did, and once Arthur was made aware of the shield's meaning he confronted Tristan who told him Morgan le Fay was behind it.

Tristan went in search of Lancelot but encountered Palomides, who was beset by nine knights. He helped his sometime enemy, and afterward they agreed to meet and joust. Riding towards Camelot for combat, Tristan chanced upon Lancelot. They fought until they recognized one another, at which point they both surrendered and rode on together. Tristan was invited again to join the Round Table, and this time accepted.

King Mark of Cornwall heard of Tristan's growing fame and decided to kill him. On the way to Camelot, he met various Knights of the Round Table and revealed his cowardly and untrustworthy nature. When he finally reached Camelot, King Mark was

BELOW: **Tristan and Palomides were often enemies, but seem to have had a degree of mutual respect. At times they fought together against a common foe; on other occasions, they made vigorous attempts to kill one another.**

forced to renounce his enmity for Tristan. Mark and Tristan went back to Cornwall together.

In Cornwall, Tristan was instrumental in saving the kingdom from invasion, and when another foe attacked soon afterwards, it was King Mark's brother Boudwin who led the victory. Mark was jealous of the renown his brother won and murdered him. His family, notably his son Alisander, escaped and planned vengeance.

King Mark then became aware of a plot to kill Lancelot at a tournament, and sent Tristan to it disguised as Lancelot. Although attacked by numerous knights, Tristan survived and won the tournament, so Mark had him drugged and imprisoned him in a castle. After twice escaping captivity, Tristan left Cornwall taking Isolde with him.

Tristan and Isolde attended a tournament at which Tristan and Palomides fought several times. Although they had been enemies and both loved the same woman, they did respect one another and remained cordial foes thereafter.

BELOW: **Tristan and Isolde meet their end in various ways, depending on the version of the story. Here, their funeral at Tintagel is depicted, attended by the villainous King Mark of Cornwall.**

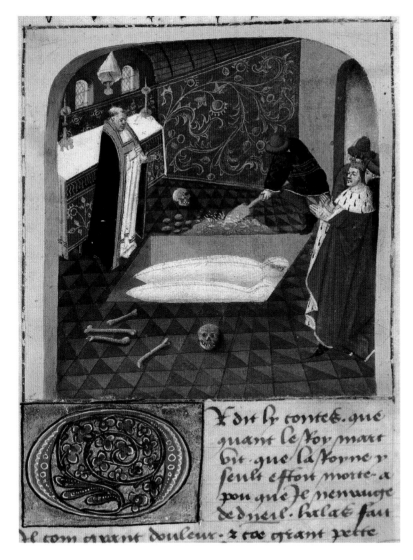

Lancelot's Sinful Ways

The drawn-out affair between Lancelot and Guinevere resumes, and continues a theme of infidelity causing serious problems throughout the tale. Arthur's conception was the result of a magically-

THE GRAIL QUEST IN MALORY

Malory's Grail Quest is broadly similar to that of previous versions. It begins with the arrival of Galahad at Camelot and his drawing of the sword from the stone. According to Malory, Merlin placed it there after taking it from Sir Balin after his death. Lancelot undergoes the same lengthy penance, but ultimately cannot complete the Grail Quest due to his sins.

Likewise, the main events of the quest are much the same – Perceval and Bors accompany Galahad as he progresses towards the Grail and finally reaches it. The ending is the same, too, and afterwards some of the knights return to Camelot. Lancelot is one of them, and despite all the efforts he made during the quest to leave his sinful ways behind, he soon resumes his adulterous relationship with Guinevere.

assisted seduction of another man's wife; his accidental incest with Morgause resulted in the birth of Mordred, who finally slew him. The adultery of Guinevere with Lancelot caused the final downfall of Arthur and the Round Table, although other tensions contributed as well.

Lancelot and Guinevere began to be increasingly careless about concealing their affair. Although some politely failed to notice what was happening, there were some who looked on with interest. Among them were Mordred and his brother Agravaine, who were not well disposed towards Arthur or those involved in the affair.

Lancelot tried to conceal his indiscretion by laying a false trail. He increasingly sought out the company of women other than Guinevere, which angered her to the point where she

THE ADULTERY OF GUINEVERE AND LANCELOT CAUSED THE FINAL DOWNFALL OF ARTHUR.

banished him from the court. Dismayed, he became a hermit. Guinevere, in the meantime, held a feast for several knights at which Sir Pinel tried to murder Gawain with poisoned fruit. This was in revenge for Gawain's slaying of Lamorak some time earlier, which was part of a blood feud that started when King Pellinore (Lamorak's father) killed King Lot. Much later, Lot's sons Gawain and Gaheris killed Pellinore in revenge.

Lamorak had an affair with King Lot's widow, Arthur's half-sister Morgause, and was caught in bed with her by Gaheris.

ABOVE: **Despite repenting of his sins, Lancelot resumed his affair with Guinevere and became increasingly blatant about it. His subsequent attempt to conceal the matter angered her.**

Gaheris slew his mother in a rage, but let Lamorak go because he was unarmed. Gawain, Gaheris, Agravaine and Mordred later attacked Lamorak; all were involved in his killing, but Mordred delivered the deathblow.

Gawain did not eat the poisoned fruit, but Sir Patrise did, and he died as a result. Guinevere was blamed for the incident and tried for murder. It was decided to fight a judicial duel to decide her guilt or innocence, but no champion came forward – the knights believed she had tried to kill them and were not inclined to defend her. Lancelot would have, of course, but he was living as a hermit after she had banished him.

Bors eventually agreed to defend Guinevere, but secretly went to find Lancelot who would make a better champion. Lancelot arrived just in time for the duel and confronted Sir Mador, a kinsman of Patrise. If Lancelot lost, Guinevere would be burned at the stake. He won the fight and was welcomed back by his comrades. Soon after, Nimue arrived at court and explained that Sir Pinel had actually poisoned the fruit. Guinevere was no longer under suspicion.

Arthur left Camelot to attend a tournament, and Lancelot followed after in disguise, since he wanted to fight without anyone being made fearful by his reputation. He agreed to wear a token of favour provided by the tournament host's daughter, Elaine, an act that angered Guinevere when she found out about it.

Lancelot defeated many knights, although he was injured in the process. Elaine asked Lancelot to marry her or take her as his lover, but he refused and she died of grief soon after he returned to Camelot. It is worth noting at this point that this Elaine was not the same one as the Grail King's daughter. Be that as it may, her body came to Camelot floating on a funeral barge, with a letter in her hand outlining her tragic death.

Guinevere was pleased that Lancelot had rejected Elaine, and the affair continued. At a Christmas tourney Guinevere asked Lancelot to wear a token of her favour, which he did. He fought in disguise, but attracted attention with his feats of arms. Even Arthur participated in this tourney.

Sir Lancelot and the Cart

Malory places the 'Knight of the Cart' incident at this point in the tale. Guinevere is captured by Meliagrance (Meleagant) while celebrating the arrival of May, and subsequent events are similar but slightly different to earlier versions of the story. Lancelot reaches Meliagrance in a chariot after his horse is killed in an ambush, rather than the cart of the earlier story. Guinevere is accused of adultery with a wounded knight of her escort rather than Sir Kay, and Lancelot is tricked into falling through a trapdoor and is held in a cave rather than a tower.

ABOVE: **After being banished from Camelot, Lancelot became a hermit. He might have remained thus, had Guinevere not been falsely accused of murdering Sir Patrise.**

Guinevere is sentenced to be burned at the stake if the accusation of adultery is proven by her champion's defeat – or, in this case, non-appearance. Lancelot manages to escape in time to fight for her and defeats Meliagrance with one hand tied behind his back. After this incident, things go on much as before.

Mordred and Agravaine threatened to reveal the affair to Arthur, although Gawain warned them that this would split the Round Table. Agravaine told him anyway, and Arthur agreed to

a trial by combat between Lancelot and Agravaine to see if the charge was true. He was also persuaded to agree to a ruse to trap Lancelot if the accusations were correct.

Arthur declared he was going hunting for a day or two, and would be away overnight. Sure enough, Lancelot did not go on the hunt. Bors warned Lancelot that it would be imprudent to go to Guinevere that night, but he went anyway and was caught in her bedchamber by Mordred accompanied by a dozen knights. Lancelot killed one of them and took his armour, demanding a fair fight on the tourney field. This was refused, so Lancelot came out of the bedchamber and attacked his enemies, killing Agravaine and all the others except Mordred.

asseure que de samort Loze sui dome sui
qil conp par vne leaume qil sui fait
entrer lespec ene pline de deux doice Et
mordree sui reprie le rsue tyant conp
qil onroues pot runiener des bras h
sente domiagent tant qil ur a reslur q
ne sout et trauaillee · mais mordree a
le rsue bel de sa meslee · si le mame sa ou
il uenst Et tant a fait qnil le met andef
soubz de lui et sui oste leaume de la teffe
et dit qil lotiua sil ne lui octroie sa vou
lente et le chenalier sui france tont errat
u fawe quant que il sui commandera Et
loze sui dist, mordree qnil sui pardoust tont
son mal tusout et cil dist, monlt voutenhers
Er il sui france Encore ce vueille fait mor
dree que tu mesiance que tu pardome
ras a ta damoiselle ton maltalent Et

il dist ques suit il · mais de ce trespassa
il son ttrant Car onroues vne, ne pot
la damoiselle aymer pour those qui
lui aneust · Au matin sen parti mor
dree et monta sur son chenalque lee
see esture sui orent apparaille et sel
met en iellerent, monlt de la bataille qui s
anoient commancerent enteulx y · car
ilz, nanoient vene ony et ce ne estoit
mie de merueilles car sa sotte estoit si
lomg qnilz, ne les penstort mie bien ow
Et qnant mordree su monte sur son
chenal si se depart du chenalier et de
la damoiselle et se met en son chemm
sicomme il anoit fait denant · Mais
atant se tuft le compte apavler le sui
et retowne apavler de son fiere aftia
name

Comment aguuam lozquilleuo fee
messire guulam, et miee le Roy artue
troua le duelque vny fuisout a vny
pauerllon pour vny chlr que driass le
felon anoit ottis · et aghranum toppa
la teffe a drias · et vne sournchie
du neuf cheftel broir de vde abbatit

aguuam, et le mit, en prison et luy
euft coppee la teffe se ne suft vne damoiss
endroit dit le compte que quat
ayrauam se su parti de ses co
paugnons sicomme vont ance
oue, qnil seua n-iours sens
Cii entre trouue avon dome ar ne tenan

As Gawain had feared, the company of the Round Table was split. Lancelot was supported by friends including Bors, and also by friends of Tristan and Lamorak who had grudges against those who were now opposed to Lancelot. Mordred went to Arthur and told him what had happened, and Arthur accepted that the charge of adultery was proven. Gawain tried to convince him that this was a mistake; Lancelot was a good friend to both Guinevere and Arthur and might have had a good reason for attending her during the night.

Arthur sentenced Guinevere to death by burning and ordered Gawain to convey her to her execution. Gawain refused, but his brothers Gareth and Gaheris went. They did not wear armour as a sign that they were not seeking a fight with other Round Table knights. Despite this, Lancelot slew them and many others in a bid to rescue Guinevere. He took her to his castle, Joyous Gard, and fortified himself there. He was soon joined by others who opposed Arthur.

Arthur besieged Joyous Gard for 15 weeks, during which Lancelot would not fight him. At length they began to speak of peace, but Gawain wanted revenge for his kinsmen. Reluctantly, Lancelot gave battle. Even then he would not strike Arthur, but defended him when he was unhorsed.

The Pope sent word that he wanted the fighting to stop,

BELOW: Lancelot's rescue of Guinevere, and his slaying of the knights escorting her to the stake, divided the Round Table and earned him the bitter enmity of Gawain. The stage was set for the final act of the tragedy.

and both Arthur and Lancelot were willing. But again Gawain pressed the quarrel. Arthur banished Lancelot from England, and Gawain approved since he could fight Lancelot overseas without being subject to Arthur's orders not to. Lancelot returned to his native France, taking with him Bors and other loyal supporters.

Arthur followed Lancelot to France with an army, but agreed to a peace parlay. Again it was Gawain who prevented peace from being made. Gawain besieged Lancelot's castle for months, issuing daily challenges, until finally Lancelot agreed to fight him. Gawain had obtained a blessing that gave him extra strength for part of the day, so Lancelot had to withstand his onslaught during this time before defeating Gawain. Lancelot spared his enemy, and so they had to fight again when Gawain had healed. Defeated again, Gawain rested and prepared for another battle.

> LANCELOT WOULD NOT STRIKE ARTHUR, AND EVEN DEFENDED HIM WHEN HE WAS UNHORSED.

The Death of Arthur

Mordred, nephew of King Arthur, was left to rule in Arthur's stead while he was on campaign in France. He declared that Arthur had been killed in battle and had himself crowned king, intending to marry Guinevere. Guinevere managed to escape from him to the Tower of London where she was besieged. Meanwhile, Mordred marched to Dover where he tried to prevent Arthur from landing his army.

Mordred's defence failed, although Gawain was mortally injured when a wound from his battle with Lancelot reopened. Before he died Gawain wrote to Lancelot begging him to come and help Arthur. He was buried at Dover, while Arthur continued to campaign against Mordred. Even after further defeats Mordred gained additional support from those who resented Arthur or had supported Lancelot.

Mordred prepared for a renewed battle at Salisbury, and Arthur was warned by Gawain in a dream that he would die if the battle was fought. He decided to seek a truce. This was agreed, and Arthur met Mordred with a handful of guards to solemnize the truce. One of the escorting knights drew his sword to deal with an adder he saw, and a fight broke out. This escalated into a full-scale battle, in which both sides lost heavily.

With only Bedivere and Lucan remaining of the Round Table knights, Arthur led a final charge at Mordred and slew him, but received a mortal wound in the process. Bedivere and Lucan got him to a chapel, but Lucan died there of his own wounds. Knowing that he was dying, Arthur told Bedivere to throw Excalibur in the nearby lake, but Bedivere was reluctant. He said he had done it, but Arthur saw through the lie and sent him back twice more until he finally did as he was bidden. Excalibur was caught by a woman's hand emerging from the lake, and thus returned to the Lady of the Lake. Four women arrived on a boat, including the Lady of the Lake, to take Arthur's body away. Among them was also Morgan le Fay, who was now reconciled with Arthur.

BELOW: A depiction of Guinevere under siege by Mordred's forces. The attackers are using a trebuchet to reduce the defences, whilst both sides shoot crossbows at one another. Siege warfare was not the stuff of heroic knightly legends.

Lancelot came to help Arthur, but arrived too late. He visited Guinevere, who had joined a convent, and she told him she did not want to see him again in life. He became a holy man, as did Bedivere. Upon hearing some years later that Guinevere had died, he went to her. She was, in fact, still alive until just before he arrived. He took her body to be buried beside Arthur's, and soon afterwards he, too, died. A few of the former Round Table knights lived on after the battle with Mordred, but the era of their fellowship was over. Constantine, son of Cador of Cornwall, became king of a diminished England.

LEFT: **Sir Bedivere reluctantly returned Excalibur to the Lady of the Lake at Arthur's behest. This echoes an ancient Sarmatian tradition that a prince's sword should be thrown into the sea when he dies.**

Malory's tale is one of tragedy, and of greatness rising from chaos and falling back again once the fellowship of the Round Table was broken. The values that made the Knights of the Round Table notable were eventually forgotten, but for those years when chivalry, piety and honour were observed, King Arthur and his knights were invincible. Even when they were gone their legend remained, a bright moment on the far side of the darkness.

Where Geoffrey of Monmouth's version is a pseudo-history that attempts to put a date on the events – even if it is riddled with anachronisms – Malory's tale makes no real pretence of fitting with historical fact. It takes place in the reign of King Arthur, a wholly mythical era somewhere before the present. More detail is not really necessary.

THE ARTHURIAN STORY STANDS ON ITS OWN MERIT; THERE IS NO NEED TO PRETEND THAT IT IS HISTORY.

6

ARTHURIAN ROMANCE TODAY

Until the sixteenth century, the work of Geoffrey of Monmouth was widely regarded as a serious and reasonably accurate history of Britain. As well as misleading historians, this made it an ideal basis for adventure stories and romances.

However, interest waned in the myths of King Arthur, and not coincidentally the legendary history of Britain faded from the scene. Malory's work was reprinted until 1634, but few tales were added to the Arthurian mythos for many years. Although the story was not forgotten, it was not until the early nineteenth century that serious interest again began to be taken in the 'Matter of Britain'. There are many possible reasons why this

OPPOSITE: The 2004 film *King Arthur* offers the 'true story behind the myth'. Whilst it is based on one of the possible 'real Arthur' candidates, its basis in history is questionable at best.

occurred, and the truth is most likely a combination of all of them. The Renaissance gave way to the Age of Enlightenment, and from there Europe progressed through increasing industrialism into an era where science and technology guided the mindset of society and produced enough marvels to inspire the soul.

Inevitably, however, there was a movement away from this obsession with the physical world, and with it came renewed interest in the Medieval and Classical eras – or more accurately a romanticized version of them. At the same time, the concept of nationhood in the modern sense was becoming prevalent across Europe.

A Hero for the Age of Industry

In a world where nations were beginning to emerge, it is hardly surprising that Britain would ask itself who it was and where it came from. The story of King Arthur, although, of course, almost completely fictional, was a compelling one. Britain was united under King Arthur, and its heroes held dear values of fellowship, courage and honour that struck a chord with the reader.

The industrial era, beginning around 1750 or so, represented an age of opportunity in which a man might enrich himself by means of industry or commerce and aspire to join the social elite. The sons of 'new money' had no traditions, no sense of belonging as members of the elite and were often snubbed by those who came from 'old money'. Tales and legends that helped create a sense of identity were likely to be highly influential.

One of the skills that a young man was expected to demonstrate was fencing. While the elegant play of the smallsword was far removed from knightly clashes with sword and shield, the young man attending fencing tuition might find parallels with tales of knights or squires in training.

The custom of duelling – although often with pistols rather than swords – was also prevalent in this era. Just as Arthur's knights tested themselves in a tourney or a pas d'armes, a young man of society might

BELOW: The smallsword is a rather different weapon to the arms of a knight, but the mystique of the sword still rings true. Even today, competitive fencers may still feel a kinship with the chivalrous swordsmen of old.

find himself forced by social custom to confront an equal in a ritualized combat. It was the trappings of noble and honourable combat that raised the duel above a mere brawl with swords, and it is not hard to see a connection stretching back to the romanticized encounters of Arthur's knights.

Social standing and appropriate conduct were also vital in this era. Just as a knight of the Middle Ages might be ruined if others thought he 'lacked honour', so a gentleman of the industrial era would suffer disgrace and financial disaster if his reputation was tarnished. While often corrupt and dissolute to a quite shocking degree, these gentlemen were as concerned about what others thought of them as any Arthurian knight. There are occasions in Malory where a knight declares that he prefers to die than accept the shame of surrender, taking his good name to the grave with him. So it was with the gentleman of this later age, who might be willing to engage in some desperate enterprise or fight a duel to preserve his own reputation.

Thus there was much in common between the society of the eighteenth- or nineteenth-century gentleman and the nobles of legend. The chivalrous values

ABOVE: **The clearly stated quarrel and the formality of the duel are little different to the confrontations of Arthurian knights, though the weapons are very different. Ceremony and honourable conduct raised the duel above a simple attempt at mutual murder.**

A KNIGHT OF THE MIDDLE AGES WOULD BE RUINED IF OTHERS THOUGHT HE LACKED HONOUR.

of Arthur's knights were not so very different to the social expectations of a gentleman in 1750, and the idea of men winning a place at the Round Table by merit and achievement may be been taken as a metaphor for finding a place in the well-established but changing society of the era.

In the late 1700s, with the French Revolution threatening to spread to other nations, the idea of a strong king and his loyal knights would have been attractive – at least to the richer classes of society. A few years later, with invasion by Napoleon's armies a real possibility, the king who fought the Saxon invaders was again a rallying point. And, of course, everyone likes a good story. All comparisons to political and social events aside, *Le Morte d'Arthur* also benefited from being that.

Arthur's Revival

Malory's *Le Morte d'Arthur* was reprinted in 1816, almost two centuries after its last edition. This spectacular revival has rarely been paralleled by any book. It was followed by new Arthurian works, such as those of Alfred, Lord Tennyson. In 1832, he published *The Lady of Shalott*, with a revised version later. From 1859 to 1885 Tennyson rewrote Malory's stories as poems that were published as *Idylls of the King*. This version was influenced by the times it was written in, much as Malory's vision of the Arthurian era was coloured by the Wars of the Roses that were ongoing as he wrote.

BELOW: Many of Richard Wagner's works were based on Germanic epic poems. *Lohrengrin* was his first Arthurian opera; it drew on the story of the Holy Grail.

Wordsworth, too, wrote Arthurian poems, such as the *Romance of the Water-Lily* (or *The Egyptian Maid*), and these works brought the tales of King Arthur back to the attention of the public. In the meantime, the Arthurian legends had caught the attention of Richard Wagner, who created operas based on Germanic and Norse legends, such as the *Nibelungenlied*.

Before Wagner wrote his famous *Der Ring des Nibelungen*, he composed *Lohengrin*, an opera based on the Perceval-Grail story and a sequel to it that featured the eponymous hero as Percival's son. Even before Wagner had finished composing his famous Ring Cycle he was working on *Tristan und Isolde*, which was, of course, based on the tragic Arthurian tale. His final completed opera, *Parsifal*, premiered in 1882. This was based on the tale of Percival and the Holy Grail as written by German poets around 1200.

Wagner's work was part of a revival of interest in Germanic/Nordic culture that included new versions of Germanic paganism and other modern takes on concepts from the Middle Ages or earlier. This came by way of cultural movements, such as Romanticism, itself a reaction to the increasingly stuffy attitudes of the Age of Enlightenment. Romanticism was fading in popularity by the later nineteenth century but despite this Wagner's works passed into popular culture, ensuring that at least some of the Arthurian stories continued to be told in new forms.

Other operatic treatments appeared in the latter years of the nineteenth century, although interest seems to have waned after the first decade of the twentieth century. There have been occasional Arthurian operas since but not many, although theatre productions and musical plays continue to appear.

One of the earliest Arthur plays is the 1691 *King Arthur* by Henry Purcell. This is a semi-opera, with some cast members singing, but the majority of the main cast speaking their lines. Other plays have featured music by composers such as Elgar and Britten.

The 1960 musical play *Camelot* was later filmed and found favour with US president John F. Kennedy, whose presidency was sometimes described as 'Camelot'. This was presumably

OPPOSITE: **Sir Alfred, Lord Tennyson is primarily famous for poems such as 'Charge of the Light Brigade', but he also published Arthurian tales and poems. These were reimaginings for the era in which Tennyson lived.**

BELOW: **Purcell's *King Arthur* is the earliest known musical play based upon the Arthurian legends. It is more based in the tales of Geoffrey of Monmouth than Malory.**

intended to refer to a golden age of strong leadership with powerful people surrounding a charismatic leader, but it also has connotations of broken fellowship and destruction by internal tensions.

Arthur plays continue to appear from time to time. Indeed, the tale of King Arthur has become not just a setting, but almost a genre in its own right. This applies to films, books and other media, as well as theatre, of course.

ABOVE: **The 1967 film** *Camelot* **is a movie production of the 1960 stage play.**

Nazis and the Holy Grail

The early twentieth century was a turbulent time. Tales of a heroic British king who fought Germanic (Saxon) invaders were appealing in an era of tension with and finally war against Germany, and, after the Great War was over, tales of heroic Britons remained at least modestly popular.

The chaos that existed in Germany after the Great War permitted various extremist political groups to gain power, and out of their struggles came the Nazi regime. Much has been made of the idea that the Nazis were driven or motivated by some dark supernatural force. This belief is perhaps comforting, inasmuch as it would allow us to believe that normal people could not be capable of such evil. However, the majority of writing on the subject is speculative or lacking in hard evidence. The reality is grimmer – the Nazis were simply bad people, who needed no supernatural assistance or urging to do evil.

However, some of the Nazi leadership did have an interest in the occult and the supernatural, and these were not the only offbeat fields that were investigated. 'Nazi super-science' has become almost a trope in some genres of fiction and video games, and certainly the Nazis were willing to experiment in areas that seem – at best – distinctly strange to our more rational viewpoint.

Many of the scientific projects they attempted might be described as extreme blue-sky research, and some went far beyond that.

Similarly, the Nazis were interested in acquiring religious, occult and historical objects. Some of them might well have believed that supernatural powers might be conferred by an ancient holy relic, but others were probably more concerned with what these items represented. Crazed and evil as they might be, the Nazis understood the power of symbology.

Thus their acquisition of ancient Celtic and Nordic religious items may not have necessarily had anything to do with using them to conjure otherworldly powers; they might have been quite content with the propaganda or cultural value of possessing items such as ancient Celtic cauldrons or the Bayeux Tapestry. The Nazis were promoting a Germanic revival, which included an interest in old Germanic lore, treasures from long ago and other cultural tokens. Any items they found would strengthen this cultural movement.

The Ahnenerbe Institute was created to find evidence that the Nazi belief in Aryan superiority was correct. To do so, it undertook anthropological, archaeological and historical research in Germany and elsewhere. The purpose of many expeditions is recorded – although there is always the possibility of a hidden agenda – but others were undertaken for unknown purposes. It is not impossible that at least some of these expeditions were searching for holy relics such as the Spear of Destiny, the Ark of the Covenant and the Holy Grail itself. To what purpose these items might have been put is a matter for speculation.

CRAZED AND EVIL AS THEY WERE, THE NAZIS UNDERSTOOD THE POWER OF SYMBOLOGY.

Expeditions were launched to regions as remote as Tibet and Antarctica, usually with plausible enough (given who was sending them) reasons. Some expeditions were of a general or specific scientific nature, some sought resources. Anthropological research was a high priority, since Hitler's scientists were trying to 'prove' that the world had always been dominated by Caucasians, notably of Nordic descent.

Although there is little in the way of hard evidence, there remains a persistent assertion that some of these expeditions were hunting for religious artefacts, and for more than cultural purposes. The idea has found its way into the general consciousness by way of films such as *Indiana Jones and the Last Crusade*, which features a Nazi expedition to find the Holy Grail.

The idea of a Nazi Grail Quest is certainly no stranger than some of the other ideas that were pursued during the run-up to World War II. However, it seems more than likely that the Nazi obsession with the occult has been greatly overstated and that any attempt to find the Grail or other religious artefacts was part of a general obsession with grabbing the best and most famous of everything. It is interesting to wonder, however, to what extent the Nazi interest in the Holy Grail was influenced or sparked by the Arthurian legends.

BELOW: Mark Twain's tale of a time-traveller at King Arthur's court might seem clichéd today, but at the time of writing it was exploring a whole new genre. Since then, all manner of people have visited Arthur's court and had a wide range of adventures.

New Directions in Fiction

In the meantime, the Arthurian legend had even found itself into the pages of the emerging science fiction genre. The author of *A Connecticut Yankee in King Arthur's Court*, Mark Twain, might not usually be associated with science fiction, but there is really no other term for a story in which a modern (for Twain's time) person is transported back to the age of King Arthur.

By way of comparison, H.G. Wells' *The Time Machine* was published in 1895, although an earlier tale named *The Chronic Argonauts* appeared in 1888 and deals with similar concepts. Twain's story came out in 1889. It is likely that the Arthurian era was used as the backdrop for the adventures of Twain's time-travelling Yankee as it would be at least vaguely familiar to the reader. With characters such as Merlin ready-made, Twain needed to spend less effort on developing them and explaining his background.

Twain's hero uses his knowledge of modern technology such as gunpowder to impress the denizens of the Medieval era, and rises to great power. When events turn against him he leads a small force equipped with Gatling guns against the might of Medieval chivalry, slaughtering knights in heaps. Twain's tale is intended as a counterpoint or satire of the tendency to romanticize the Middle Ages. The legends of King Arthur made an ideal target for such an endeavour.

The concept of some inappropriate person being deposited in an earlier era has been used repeatedly, with everything from spacemen to disguised robots sent back to the time of King Arthur. Other variants of the tale have alluded to the original without making any attempt to fit with its story or characters. Among these is the 1992 film *Evil Dead III: Army of Darkness*, in which the time-travelling hero helps Lord Arthur defeat an undead army.

The Arthur story has inspired a great many novels. Some are fairly straight retellings of the Arthur story, although usually with some new elements or a different perspective. *The Once and Future King*, by T.H. White features a Merlin who experiences time in reverse. His foreknowledge is nothing more than memory of what are to him past events. Rosemary Sutcliff's Arthurian novels tie in with her *Eagle of the Ninth* series, linking Arthur to events in the Roman era.

Marion Zimmer Bradley's *The Mists of Avalon* tells the tale from the point of view of the major female players – characters who were given little attention in the original tales – while Mary Stewart's Merlin trilogy is from the point of view of Merlin, but followed by a sequel in which the protagonist is Mordred.

Some novels tread the line between historical fiction and fantasy. David Drake, David Gemmel and Bernard Cornwall have all written pseudo-historical tales about King Arthur that focus on his wars and campaigns. Pseudo-historical versions of the Arthur legend tend to be set around 400–600 AD, the era in which Arthur

EVERYTHING FROM SPACEMEN TO DISGUISED ROBOTS HAVE BEEN SENT BACK TO KING ARTHUR'S ERA.

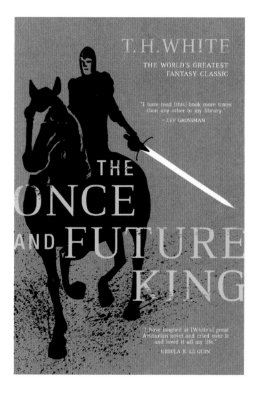

T.H.WHITE
THE WORLD'S GREATEST FANTASY CLASSIC

"I have read [this] book more times than any other in my library."
– LEV GROSSMAN

THE ONCE AND FUTURE KING

"I have laughed at [White's] great Arthurian novel and cried over it and loved it all my life."
URSULA K. LE GUIN

ABOVE: Novels give the author more room to explore new concepts and develop characters. In *The Once and Future King*, Merlin experiences time in reverse and remembers the future.

COMIC CHARACTERS

Arthurian characters have also been highly influential in comic books and graphic novels. Marvel Comics ran a series with time-travelling mutant heroes at King Arthur's court, while DC Comics has also run stories about Arthur and his companions. Some of the graphic versions of the Arthur story are quite different from the originals, including one in which the reincarnated Knights of the Round Table battle aliens in 3000 ad. Excalibur proves capable of cutting anything – including atoms – and thereby causes an atomic explosion.

was supposed to have lived, and therefore eschew Medieval technology and social conventions for a more realistic portrayal of the 'Dark Ages'. There are exceptions, of course, but most attempts to portray Arthur as a historical figure are set in this era.

Some of the more radical reinventions of the Arthur story involve reincarnated Arthurian characters in the modern world or an Arthur awoken from his long sleep in Avalon. In *Knight Life* by Peter David, Arthur awakens in time to run for mayor in modern-day New York, receiving Excalibur from the Lady of the Lake in Central Park.

Other tales merely allude to the Arthur story or mention it in passing. The children's novel *The Weirdstone of Brisingamen* borrows liberally from Norse and Celtic mythology, and is based around the legend of a wizard who guards a sleeping king and his knights. The Changes trilogy, of which *The Weathermonger* is the most well known, is set in a future where people fear technology and have returned to a Medieval way of life due to the influence of Merlin.

Early Twentieth-Century Films

There have, of course, been a great many films that either tell part or all of the Arthur story, or at least borrow from it. The earliest is an adaptation of Wagner's opera *Parsifal*, which opened at the box office in 1904. Numerous film adaptations followed, of which some were based on the existing tales and others on new stories hung on characters with a familiar name.

The tale of Lancelot and Guinevere seems to have a particular fascination for film-makers. Some, such as the 1963 *Lancelot and Guinevere*, are specifically about these two characters while others (for example the 1953 *Knights of the Round Table*) tell a wider story based upon Malory's work, but inevitably tend to have Lancelot and Guinevere among the main characters.

Some of these Arthurian films were made on an extremely low budget or in amateurish fashion, reusing generic 'knight movie' props or specific and distinctive items from other films. Some actually recycled footage from other films. Although there were some creditable efforts, the regular appearance of fairly low-quality Arthur films may well have been a factor in creating the 1975 *Monty Python and the Holy Grail*. A spoof is only funny, after all, if it is poking fun at something familiar.

In addition to the downright silly, the Arthurian film genre has spawned adaptations that were unusual or just plain strange. The 1978 *Perceval de Gallois* is a telling of the original Chrétien de Troyes Grail legend that combines elements of the original text with deliberately basic theatricality. The 1982 *Parsifal* is a performance of Wagner's opera that includes allusions to the Nazi interest in Wagner's work, essentially incorporating the story of the legend into the performance.

ABOVE: The 1963 *Lancelot and Guinevere* was one of many films exploring or based around the Lancelot-Guinevere-Arthur love triangle. This seems to be one of the most enduring stories of all time.

There were also serials featuring Arthurian characters. In the 1940s and 1950s most serials were Westerns, although science fiction was also popular. Period, or perhaps 'fantasy' might be a better word, serials were uncommon. Nevertheless, *The Adventures of Sir Galahad* appeared in cinemas from 1949, and *The Adventures of Sir Lancelot* was screened on television in 1956.

Games, Animation and Music

The Arthurian mythos provides a rich backdrop – and ready-made characters – for games. In some cases, this is a simple shortcut – a knight character can be identified as Lancelot or a wizard as Merlin without any real need for explanation. Some games revolve around the Arthurian characters, although the style varies from complex strategy to marching sideways along a scrolling landscape chopping down enemies who dutifully rush up to be dispatched.

Arthur and his knights appear in a number of multiplayer online games, often in ways that suggest little research has been done. Typically the 'Arthur characters' who appear in such games are fairly generic representations of the popular conception of the knights, sometimes with quite bizarre quirks and alterations. However, perhaps the oddest reimagining to date has Sonic the Hedgehog battling to save Camelot and becoming its king.

THE TREATMENT OF ARTHURIAN CHARACTERS OFTEN SUGGESTS A LACK OF RESEARCH.

The roleplaying game *Pendragon* treats the Arthurian mythos a little more respectfully. In this game, players take on the role of knights in a world that attempts to rationalize the many versions of the Arthur story. One way this is done is to use distinct phases, so a game might be set during Arthur's early reign and have a different feel to one set during the Grail Quest. New technology is introduced as the game's timeline moves forward.

One key element of the *Pendragon* game is the way it portrays the personalities of characters through paired and rated traits. So a knight who is extremely generous will have relatively little difficulty passing a challenge in which he has the chance to be greedy; a character with the vice of being cowardly is less likely to stand and face his foe when things are going badly than one who is known for his valour.

BELOW: The roleplaying game Pendragon makes a very creditable effort at reconciling the many versions of the tale into a single timeline yet still reflecting the different aspects of the Arthurian mythos.

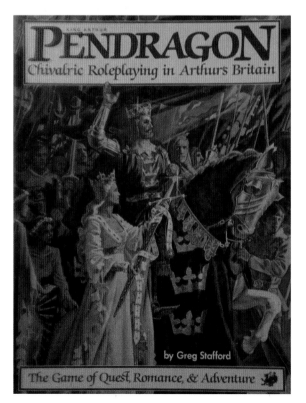

These traits, combined with the character's loves, hates and passions (such as loyalty, honour or love of a particular person) also indicate the chance that a knight will become inspired to perform great deeds. These game mechanics do a very good job of allowing players to create their own Arthurian adventures.

As well as video and over-the-table games, the Arthur story has been presented in various animated forms. Most famous of these is the 1963 Disney

ARTHUR PUT TO MUSIC

The legend of King Arthur has also inspired numerous musical compositions other than those used in operas and musical plays. Many of these compositions are hard rock or heavy metal, with songs often relating events from the Arthurian legends or alluding to them. Band and album names, such as Roxy Music's *Avalon* and Rick Wakeman's *The Myths and Legends of King Arthur and the Knights of the Round Table,* have also been inspired by the Arthurian mythos. The amount of actual knowledge that goes into these efforts can vary considerably, but there are some cases of rock songs providing a pretty useful synopsis of the original legend.

LEFT: Rick Wakeman's *King Arthur* is one example of modern music influenced by the Arthurian mythos.

animated film *The Sword in the Stone*, which is based on a 1938 novel forming part of the 'Once and Future King' cycle. Among the more bizarre animated interpretations is the tale of an American Football team 'borrowed' from the future by Merlin when Arthur and his knights are captured.

The Legend of Prince Valiant is rather more mainstream, dealing with the adventures of young squires training to become Knights of the Round Table. It is derived from the comic strip of the same name that was first published in 1937 and was also developed into a video game.

Later Films and Television Adaptations

There have been many documentaries about Arthur and related subjects. It says a lot about how influential the story is that so many attempts have been made to 'reveal the real King Arthur'. This seems unlikely to ever end; there will always be new revelations or theories as long as the Arthur story retains the public interest.

ABOVE: **The TV series** *Camelot* **benefits from modern production values and budgets. Presented much like a 'real' historical drama, shows of this sort do not need to recycle old props and costumes in the way that many earlier productions did.**

Television adaptations likewise keep returning to the same concepts, although treating them in a different way each time. The 1998 series *Merlin* differs considerably from the 2008 version, which revolves around the relationship of a young Arthur and Merlin, as well as youthful versions of other characters from the legends.

Some television adaptations are derived from books, such as the televised version of Marion Zimmer Bradly's *Mists of Avalon*. Others, such as *Camelot*, are presented more as historical drama than a tale of fantasy, and follow a similar style to dramas set in ancient Rome or the court of Henry VIII of England. Given the nature of historical drama, shows like *Camelot* are not always that much less firmly rooted in historical fact than those that purport to represent people who actually lived.

It is through films that most people today are brought into contact with the Arthur story, and, as with other genres, the story is sufficiently compelling that new versions continue to be made. Some are presented as historical, some as a retelling of the Arthur story (i.e. that written by Malory), and some focus on elements drawn from the Arthur mythos without really being connected with it.

By way of example, several films feature wizards taught by Merlin or items possessed by him without really explaining all that much about who he was. This Merlin-of-the-backstory is represented as good or bad according to the requirements of the plot. The popularity of the Arthur story is such that an entirely unrelated film can explain a magical device as 'created by Merlin' and not need to say much more for the reader to understand and accept it. This influence is subtle, but very widespread.

AN ENTIRELY UNRELATED FILM CAN PRESENT AN ITEM AS 'CREATED BY MERLIN' WITHOUT NEEDING TO EXPLAIN FURTHER.

Perhaps the most influential film adaptation is *Excalibur*, released in 1981. It tells a somewhat adapted version of the Malory tale in a dramatic and visually striking manner. *Excalibur* may well be responsible for shaping what many people know about the Arthurian legends, and contains many of the defining concepts of the Arthur mythos, such as Arthur's conception, the romance between Lancelot and Guinevere and the mystical origins of Excalibur itself. The idea of wandering knights testing themselves by blocking a bridge or road and fighting anyone who comes by is also portrayed.

Arthur's death in *Excalibur* is suitably dramatic. Impaled on a spear by Mordred, Arthur drags himself along the shaft to get

LEFT: The movie *Excalibur* follows the Arthurian tradition of graphic violence and lurid fight scenes. The media have changed in the past few centuries, but the style of storytelling is faithfully preserved.

close enough to strike his enemy down. The film ends with the return of Excalibur to the Lady of the Lake and Arthur's body being taken away to Avalon.

While Excalibur attempted a modern-day retelling of the Malory tale, other films borrowed bits of the Arthur mythos and built a story around them. *First Knight*, released in 1995, is one such. It uses the idea of a romance between Lancelot and Guinevere, and her abduction by Meleagant, but tells an entirely new tale in which Arthur is killed by Meleagant's men and blesses Lancelot and Guinevere's love as he dies. The symbology of a disarmed Lancelot taking up Arthur's sword to defeat Meleagant is in keeping with the romantic Arthur legend, but otherwise the film has little to do with the Arthur mythos, other than borrowing some names and an idea for a plot.

The 1997 *Prince Valiant* is another example of a film that borrows a few names from the Arthur story. Vikings serving Morgan le Fay steal Excalibur, forcing a young squire to try to retrieve it. This could be any magical sword, any sorceress and any generic group of baddies; the Arthur connection was

BELOW: *First Knight* returns to the style of the earliest Arthur tales in that it has no mystical or supernatural elements, but otherwise has little more in common with the original than a few characters.

LEFT: The movie *Excalibur* is one of the finest attempts to bring the grandeur of the Arthur legend to the screen.

presumably an attempt to tie in (cynics might say cash in) on the popularity of the Arthur legends. This sort of co-opting of characters and events from the Arthur story is one reason why many people are very confused about the details of the actual tale – as if those were not confusing enough!

Other films have tried to present themselves as the true story that inspired the Arthur myths. These include *King Arthur* (2004), which portrays Arthur as a Romano-British officer defending his people after the Roman withdrawal of 467 AD. Since the Roman withdrawal historically occurred 50 years earlier, the promise of a true story seems to be on shaky ground right from the start. It is rather loosely based on the idea of Arthur as a leader of Sarmatian cavalry deployed to Britain by the Roman Empire, but is riddled with anachronisms.

Arthur in Modern Popular Culture

The Arthur story simply will not go away. It has taken root in
popular culture and elements of it have influenced or been used
in other stories far beyond pseudo-historical tales of knights in
armour. The Arthur legend has been transplanted to the modern
day and even the far future; people from today have been sent to
Arthur's court. 'The truth behind the legend' has been revealed
on several occasions both in documentary and fictional form.
The story has been told from alternative perspectives; sequels and
prequels have been created.

These tales have been told in every possible medium. The
written word and the theatre were the only media when the
Arthur story was first penned, but as
graphic novels, video games, animation,
films and television series became a
possibility, the Arthur legends were
inevitably the subject of new productions.

**THE ARTHUR STORY IS ONE
OF THE MOST ENDURING
TALES EVER WRITTEN.**

The theatrical tradition continues
to this day, with musicals based around the life of Arthur or
characters from his tales such as Merlin continuing to appear.
Some of these are a little oddball – the musical *Spamalot* is a
parody of the Arthurian legends derived from the Monty Python
film *Monty Python and the Holy Grail* that incorporates elements
from other Python films unrelated to the Arthur story. Geoffrey
of Monmouth or Thomas Malory might go mad and run off
into the forest to be a wild man at seeing their work treated this
way… or they might consider it a compliment that their stories
were popular enough to be parodied several centuries later.

At the time of writing, a new set of Arthur films is beginning
production. A six-film series is planned, presumably spanning
the entire Arthurian legend and possibly beyond. The Arthur
story is one of the most enduring tales ever written. The
reasons why are complex, and must include the fact that it is an
entertaining story. The legend of a king who brought justice and
fought to defend his people is one of those stories that makes
sense to everyone, and the fact that Arthur and his companions
were imperfect also strikes a chord. There is also something
compelling about the idea of a fallen hero who may yet some day

return when the need is greatest. There is something delightfully clear-cut about the knight who faces his foes head-on and declares his quarrel, and who will not retreat no matter how poor the odds. In a complex and deceitful world, Arthur's knights (mostly) stand as an example of honourable and straightforward conduct. Even villains keep their word and – usually – fight fair. Thus in an Arthurian world it is possible to win or lose by your own efforts rather than struggling through a morass of compromises and half-truths.

Perhaps we all would like to believe in the heroic knight-errant who comes charging to the rescue at just the right moment, and who gives aid simply because it is asked for. It may be that we are romantic enough to believe in heroes, yet realistic enough to require them to be tragic ones. If so, then the Arthur story provides us with just what we need.

Whatever the reasons, a story that was first written in 1136 – and which quite likely had its roots in much earlier tales – remains compelling today. There is a moment in one of the tales where Arthur tells his followers that if they cannot win the battle, and if everything they have built collapses into darkness, then at least they will have created a moment so bright that it will be seen on the far side of that darkness.

It would appear that he was right.

LEFT: The musical *Spamalot* may be a bit irreverent but it would not be funny if the subject were unfamiliar. The Arthur story will continue to be reimagined, reworked, retold and occasionally parodied for many years to come.

INDEX

PICTURE CREDITS